Zhaul had just wanted a night of fun . . . away from the re-
sponsibilities of his panda sleuth. Accepting the offer of a
back-room hook-up from the wrong person landed him in a
cage as a science experiment. Upon being rescued, Zhaul is
devastated to learn that no one in his sleuth had even reported
him missing. Meeting his mate lifts his spirits. Learning that
the black bear shifter has been be-spelled by witches, Zhaul
thinks perhaps Fate is laughing at him. The alpha of the
shifter gang who'd rescued him as well as his mate — Kontra
and Tim — assure him that there is a way to break the spell,
and they'll do everything in their power to help him find it.
Then he discovers a way to connect with his mate — climbing
trees. Can Zhaul discover how to build on that before those
who'd held him captive come calling?

Illuminating his Bear
Copyright © 2021 Charlie Richards
ISBN: 978-1-4874-3439-7
Cover art by Angela Waters

Published by eXtasy Books Inc

Look for us online at:
www.eXtasybooks.com

Illuminating his Bear
Kontra's Menagerie 31

By

Charlie Richards

DEDICATION

Patience is bitter, but its fruit is sweet.
~Aristotle

CHAPTER ONE

"I'm sorry." Zhaul scowled at Tim, the alpha-mate of the shifter gang that had rescued him. Disbelief flooded him. "What did you just say?"

"Your mate is in the next room."

Yup, that's what I thought he'd said.

Rubbing one palm over his jeans-clad thigh, Zhaul used his other to scrub his short, neatly trimmed beard. It had felt so good to be able to shave. The asshole scientists who'd trapped him in animal form hadn't allowed him any human decency.

And all because I wanted a fun night away from my sleuth.

Pushing those thoughts out of his mind, Zhaul nibbled his bottom lip for a moment, trying to make proper sense of Tim's words. "But only *I* can recognize my mate," he began slowly, parsing out what confused him the most. Meeting the male's compassion-filled hazel eyes, Zhaul asked, "How could *you* possibly know my mate is in the next room?"

"I had a vision," Tim answered simply. He glanced over his shoulder at Kontra—a massive grizzly shifter and the leader of the gang—and gave his man a tight smile before returning his attention to Zhaul. "But I don't know which one in there is your mate, so you'll have to let us know." After another second of hesitation, Tim added, "And it'll be interesting to see how he reacts."

Zhaul felt more confused than ever. His mind reeled with the information dump Tim and Kontra had laid on him that day. He wasn't entirely certain that, after everything that had happened, he was ready to meet his mate.

Except, finding my mate is a gift, no matter the rotten timing.

Besides, maybe this is Fate's way of apologizing for giving me a shit family.

As much as Zhaul didn't want to think about it, he couldn't get everything to stop swirling through his head. He'd lain in that cage for almost six months — he'd learned that once he'd been rescued — thinking about what he could have possibly missed about the man who he'd followed into the alley for a quickie. Zhaul didn't know what he'd done to give away the fact that he was a shifter or how the twink even knew about shifters, to begin with.

Zhaul supposed it didn't matter. He'd been hit with a tranq dart before the door had even finished closing behind him. The twink had sneered at Zhaul as he'd fallen, calling him a freak. Then the blond had backed up and watched with a smug look on his face as men in black shirts and camo pants had carried him off. Zhaul had woken in animal form in a cage, and he'd been there until Kontra and his men had rescued him.

And now I know I wasn't even reported missing by my sleuth. Bastards.

While Zhaul had known his family had been disappointed in him when he'd come out as gay, never would he have thought they would just ignore the fact that he was gone. Well, to be fair, he supposed he wouldn't put it past his father and alpha. His mother and older brother, however, surely they would have gone around them to notify . . . someone?

Should I try to find them? Or leave it lie?

"Zhaul?"

Yuma's gentle voice murmuring his name pulled Zhaul out of his thoughts. He turned to stare at the little penguin shifter sitting on the bed beside him. The pretty man peered at him with worry in his big brown eyes.

Swallowing hard, Zhaul asked, "Why are you curious about how my mate reacts?" He would worry about family shit later — if at all. A thought flickered through his mind. "Has he already acted homophobic?"

Kontra's entire gang — over two dozen men — was comprised of a bunch of mated gay couples. If one of the bear shifters in the next room had already expressed a bigoted opinion, then Zhaul hoped that man didn't end up being his mate. Plus, why would they be in the house if they did have a problem with homosexuals?

Unless they're rescued shifters like me . . .

Currently, the gang had set up their home base in the home of Olson Caynar. He'd volunteered the use of his home, and since it was deep in the bayou and easily defendable, Kontra had taken him up on his offer. Besides, it gave the guys something to do — fixing up the old place — while some of them strategized on how to infiltrate and take out other facilities. It also gave those rescued a chance to recover.

For a short while, Olson had been a guard at the facility where Zhaul had been held. The human had quit after seeing one-too-many questionable things. Zhaul had heard that Olson felt guilty for not reporting the place to the authorities, but Zhaul didn't think that would have helped, anyway.

Since joining Kontra's people, Zhaul had learned how the facilities were supposed to be a secret — an extension of a government conspiracy.

"No, they don't say anything at all, actually," Kontra told him, rubbing his fingers along the edge of his goatee. "There's six of them in there. They're in bear form, and they were bespelled by a circle of witches." Scowling, Kontra shook his head. "What is it with some people?"

"Power can corrupt," Tim commented softly. Peering over his shoulder at Kontra, he murmured, "Not everyone can be as awesome as you, my mate."

Kontra scoffed, his lips twitching. "Not awesome, but thanks, babe."

Tim returned his focus to Zhaul and stage whispered, "He

really is awesome." As Kontra snorted while pinning a fond look Tim's way, his mate continued, "Anyway, are you ready to go meet these guys? My vision showed a bear shifting, then you being held by a good-looking brown-skinned guy with a beard." Rising to his feet, Tim shrugged. "I just can't tell which bear it is, so let us know."

Zhaul's nerves flared as he rose to his feet. Anticipation mixed with uneasiness. His heart thundered in his chest, and he rubbed a hand over it absently.

"This is totally going to be a good thing," Yuma encouraged with a grin, standing beside him and gripping his forearm in a supportive hold. "I bet meeting you will totally break the spell, and you'll live happily ever after."

Hunter—Yuma's human mate—chuckled softly as he slung his arm around his lover's waist. "I love your romantic heart, honey."

Yuma beamed at Hunter, his love for his human shining in the depths of his eyes.

Zhaul glanced between the two mated pairs, knowing he wanted a love like they had.

There's only one way to get it.

After taking a deep breath, Zhaul forced a smile and nodded. "Let's see what happens."

As Zhaul followed Yuma and Hunter from the room, Kontra patted him on the shoulder and stated, "Good man. Finding your mate is a gift, no matter the how, why, or where."

Nodding once, Zhaul asked curiously, "How'd they end up here?"

"Death dropped them off," Kontra replied.

"D-Death?" Zhaul paused in the hallway and peered at the other bear shifter in confusion—while Zhaul shared his psyche with a giant panda bear, Kontra was a grizzly shifter. The male's natural dominance made it easy to defer to him, but he couldn't contain his curiosity. "Death?"

Fortunately, Kontra didn't seem to mind when people

asked for clarification. "Yeah, Death as in one of the Four Horsemen of the Apocalypse," he told him with a grin. "Guess he and his brothers are clearing out witches dealing in blood magick." Pointing at the door to Zhaul's left, Kontra revealed with a growl in his voice, "Which is how these bear shifters were subjugated."

Zhaul stared at Kontra in shock. "H-Horsemen of the A-Apocalypse?" He whispered the words. "Y-You're on"—he gulped—"like, actual speaking terms with . . . *them?*"

Holy fucking shit!

Kontra rested his hand on Zhaul's nape and massaged lightly. "They're just paranormals like us," he rumbled soothingly. "They do their job and live their lives, just like we do. There's nothing to be scared of."

Blowing out a breath, Zhaul leaned into the alpha bear's touch, allowing it to soothe and ground him. The fact that Kontra didn't seem to think anything of conversing with such powerful beings absolutely blew his mind. He'd heard tales of the paranormal creatures that controlled demons—*fucking demons*—and they were always cautionary.

You did not want to get on their radar . . . for any reason.

Yet, Kontra didn't seem to view them in the same light.

Huh. Well, considering my sleuth didn't bother reporting me missing, maybe I shouldn't believe their views anymore.

Just as that thought drifted through his mind, a melodious tenor voice echoed through the hall.

"My brother said you had a unique view of us."

A tall, slender, pale-featured male appeared ten feet away. His light-brown leather pants molded to his legs, as was his tan tunic, showcasing a muscular body. He stared at them with ice-blue eyes, and the tilt of his chin gave him a slightly haughty expression.

"You are a fascinating alpha."

Narrowing his eyes, Kontra rumbled, "Well, I just think everyone should be judged on the merits of their character," he began slowly. He tipped his head to the side just a smidge as he continued, "I apologize. I'm not certain if you're Pestilence or Famine."

In the blink of an eye, a small sheath of wheat appeared in the man's hand.

Kontra nodded once. "Famine. I'm honored to make your acquaintance."

Famine smirked at them. "It is an honor, isn't it?"

"How'd you know he's Famine?" Tim whispered, although, from the way the horseman's brow twitched just a little, Zhaul would bet the guy had heard him.

Even as Zhaul wondered the same thing, his dry mouth and the tendrils of fear snaking through his system rendered him speechless.

Kontra didn't have that problem. Pointing at the wheat, he stated, "Pestilence's weapon of choice is a hunter's bow."

Dipping his head in confirmation, Famine stated, "Death told me you're a very perceptive alpha. I'm pleased he spoke the truth."

Releasing Zhaul's nape, Kontra wrapped that arm around Tim's waist, tucking him close to his side. "I also find that when a horseman shows up, it's because they need or want something." His smile turned rueful. "What can I do for you, Famine?"

Smiling faintly, Famine revealed, "Death told me he dropped off the bears to you."

"He did," Kontra confirmed, pointing toward the door. "Now that Zhaul is no longer stuck in his panda form, we're going to introduce them."

"Then you have experience with shifters stuck in their animal form?"

Kontra nodded. "Sadly, yes."

Famine flicked his fingers, and the sheath of wheat disappeared. Then he crossed his arms over his chest. "Well, I find myself with five shifters in that very same situation," Famine told them. "Would you be willing to take them on?" Lifting a hand, he waved toward the window near the end of the hall. "With how secluded this place is, I figure an elephant, a camel, or a capybara won't be noticed until they can shift once more."

With his brows shooting up, Kontra barked a laugh. "A capybara? Aren't those the animals that sort of look like giant moles, but they're semi-aquatic?"

Nodding, Famine replied, "The very same." Again, he peered out the window. "With this place being in the swamp, I bet he'll love it here."

"Are they be-spelled, too?" Kontra asked.

Shaking his head, Famine told him, "I do not believe so. Had something injected into them or was fed something."

"When Emmett was stuck in animal form, he was fed it in his grain," Yuma revealed, referring to a white buffalo shifter. "Once he was no longer being fed it, he was able to shift again."

Famine dipped his head in acknowledgment. "I do hope that will be the case for these animals."

"You said five," Kontra pointed out. "What are the other two animals?"

"A gray wolf and a coral snake," Famine replied.

"All right," Kontra agreed. "We'll keep them safe if they don't have a problem staying with a gay motorcycle gang."

"Thank you." Famine appeared relieved. "I will bring them post-haste."

Kontra pointed toward the closed door. "Give us a few, huh? Zhaul still has to meet his mate."

"Ah." Famine's brows shot up. "This, I'm interested in see-ing." Then he moved closer, as if it would be a show.

Zhaul sure as hell hoped not as he refocused on the door.

Kontra reached past him and opened it, then led the way

Charlie Richards

inside.

After feeling Yuma give his arm another squeeze of encouragement, Zhaul followed the alpha. Immediately, his senses were swamped by the most amazing earthy scent. His blood fired in his veins, and his stomach tightened.

Yes, my mate is truly in here.

Sweeping his gaze over the six sitting brown bears, Zhaul just had to figure out which one.

CHAPTER TWO

Congo sat in the room . . . waiting. Although it was a bit hot for his bear form, he hadn't been ordered to shift. Instead, someone had asked him if he could shift.

Really, what kind of question was that? I'm a shifter. Of course I can shift.

Not to mention, since Congo had been in his brown bear form, it wasn't as if he could actually answer. So, he'd remained still. After all, it could have been a trap.

When the witches had first begun training Congo and his men, they would do that on occasion. They would make comments that seemed to be questions when they were in animal form. Then, if they tried to answer them, they were punished.

Now, Congo knew better.

Only respond to direct orders.

As soon as the grizzly shifter and his weird-smelling mate had left the room—Congo recognized the distinctive scent of magick flowing off the male, so he knew to stay in line—Congo had crept carefully to the window, all the while ignoring the pinpricks of fiery pain that licked through his muscles due to moving without permission. He'd spotted lots of activity in the expansive yard—men moving to and fro, carrying wood, windows, and tools. Congo had also noticed a hyena sitting at the edge of the cypress forest, nearly fifty feet away.

The shifter had been staring directly at his window.

Congo had rumbled in annoyance as he settled back against the wall. Sweeping his gaze over the other five bears, he silently mourned for those who were missing—another six males that he'd spent varying numbers of decades with. Even as Congo understood that the life they'd been forced into by magick-wielders was a hard one—and not one of his choosing—that didn't change the fact that he had been friends with those people.

They'd followed my lead, and now they're dead.

Even as Congo thought that, his bear grumbled angrily in his mind. He silently agreed with the other half of his psyche. Their lives completely sucked, but even as their alpha, he didn't know how to change it.

Fucking magick-wielding assholes.

Good thing they can't read minds.

Even as Congo followed their orders, he mentally railed against them. He did as he was told, sure—half because he was compelled magickally to do so, but also because of conditioning—but that didn't mean he liked it. Congo answered to their commands, but it hadn't always been that way.

Once upon a time, Congo had led his people. While they hadn't been prosperous, they had known free will. Perhaps hiding in the woods away from ... well ... everything and everyone ... hadn't been the greatest idea. Still, for over a century, it had worked.

Then the fucking witches.

Congo still had no idea how the circle of witches had not only tracked them but had learned magick capable of bending them to their will. He hadn't known such a thing existed. His mind remained in-tact, but he felt ... compelled ... coerced ... mentally to obey them. From the way his people behaved, Congo knew he wasn't alone in that need. Plus, the agony of disobedience could only be ignored for so long.

Still, they'd never been able to touch his mind—his inner thoughts—his true self.

Unfortunately, Congo couldn't act on his desires—namely, to rip out the throat of every witch in the circle.

Congo didn't know how long he sat in that room before he

heard the rumble of voices outside the door. His excellent hearing allowed him to make out most of the conversation—more shifters were being brought to these guys. Sadness filled him that more were about to be subjugated.

Then the door opened.

The grizzly shifter led a group into the room.

Congo noticed the way the male—Kontra, he'd said his name was—had a possessive arm wrapped around the magick-wielder. He wondered if the grizzly was being coerced as he was. Congo couldn't figure out another reason for him to side with those who used magick, even if it was a warlock as opposed to witches.

"Okay," Kontra began. "Here's our troubled brown bears." He peered around at them all, a concerned glint in his dark eyes. "Scent anyone you like?" As Kontra asked the question, he turned his attention to the third person who'd joined them in the room.

Upon spotting the large yet timid-looking male, Congo couldn't help but perk up with interest. The man was broad-shouldered and thickly built, with a spare tire around his middle that just made him appear sturdier.

Great for holding on and fucking.

Damn. Where did that thought come from?

Congo hadn't felt a sexual impulse since months before they'd been taken by the witches, and he didn't know where it was coming from now.

Taking in the stranger's soulful, honey-brown eyes, Congo also had a desire to take away the slightly haunted look he found within their depths. His dark hair hung around his face in waves, and there was a slight salt and pepper look to it, giving him a hint of age that belied his boy-next-door features. When the man's gaze swept over them all, Congo wanted to roar and demand his full attention.

He even found himself shifting his weight a little, ignoring the pinpricks the movement caused.

Finally, the stranger's scent hit him.

Mate!

The reason for his infatuation became crystal clear.

Oh, fucking hell. My mate is here?

Congo's pulse skyrocketed as questions he couldn't voice snapped through his mind.

What's he doing here? Is he a prisoner, too? Is he helping the warlock? Why would Fate do this to me?

"One of them, definitely," the handsome stranger claimed, looking uncertain. He glanced around at everyone again, then focused on Kontra. "But with so many smells in here, I can't tell." His dark brows furrowed as he nibbled on his bottom lip. "Um, is it safe to, uh, get close and sniff each bear?" Grimacing, he added, "Gods, that sounds so rude."

Kontra shrugged. "Once your mate is established, Zhaul, I don't think he'll mind." Clapping his free hand on Congo's mate's shoulder, Kontra offered, "We could all head outside . . . get some fresh air and sun."

Zhaul, what a gorgeous name.

Seeing Kontra's hands on Zhaul, Congo barely managed to resist lunging at the other bear. He couldn't quite stop the rumble from escaping him, though. Pain erupted up his throat and into his head, forcing him to cease the noise.

Still, it drew the attention of all three men.

Shit.

"Well, hell." Tim grinned—actually *grinned*—and it didn't appear malicious. Instead, the warlock appeared . . . happy.

Never a good thing to make a warlock happy.

"It seems one of our bears is feeling a little territorial," Tim commented.

"At least something in them isn't fucked up, then."

Kontra's words confused Congo.

Then the alpha added, "It seems the witch's spells can't disrupt a mate-pull."

"I think outside is still a good idea," Tim stated, frowning.

"Why'd we stick six bears in here anyway?"

Shrugging, Kontra stated, "Worried about them running, but from the way they move, I don't think they're able to."

Tim shook his head. "Definitely not." Then he clapped his hands. "Okay, bears. Let's go outside." As the other five bears began moving, Tim and Kontra shifted toward the wall, out of their way, so they could get by. Tim also touched Zhaul's upper arm. "Why don't you stick close to the bear that growled? I bet he's your mate."

Zhaul appeared uncertain, but he nodded.

With the order to go outside compelling him, Congo used it to his advantage. As he ambled toward the door, he slid between Zhaul and Kontra, pushing his mate away from the other bear. Congo didn't miss the worried expression on Zhaul's face, but he still continued to urge him away from the others and to head out the door before him.

Congo recalled the layout of the massive—if a bit run-down—Victorian home from when they'd been brought inside. Turning to the left, he headed toward the stairs and the front door. He exited just in time to see the five members of his sleuth fan out and stop as soon as they hit the patchy grass at the bottom of the steps.

They were outside. The order was finished.

Even as Congo wished he could urge them all into the trees, to run from the warlock and not stop, he knew he couldn't. Hell, as soon as his paws hit the dirt, he felt that same pull. His body became sluggish, and pinpricks of pain started radiating through each muscle he continued to move.

Congo fought through it enough to maneuver Zhaul a couple of steps farther from the house, but then the excruciating agony fired more insistently through him. Gritting his teeth, he stopped with his shoulder pressed against Zhaul's body. As much as he wanted to wrap the man in his arms and keep him close, he couldn't keep moving without passing out from the agony.

"Wow, they took that very literally," Tim commented, drawing Congo's attention. His brows were furrowed, and his arms were crossed over his chest. Cocking his head, Tim peered up at Kontra. "Do you think that's the key?"

"Could be," Kontra rumbled in response. "But we'll have to be damn careful how we word shit."

Tim nodded slowly, his brows still furrowed.

"And they seem to respond the best from you," Kontra continued, scowling. It was obvious the wheels in the grizzly shifter's brain were turning.

"I have a theory on that," another man stated, joining the pair on the porch.

From the guy's scent, Congo knew he was another warlock.

Just great.

The man's pale blue eyes swept over the group, and a small smile curved his lips as his focus landed on Zhaul. "Congratulations, Zhaul. I hope the pull of mating will assist us with your bear."

Zhaul hesitated a few seconds, then rested his palm on Congo's shoulder. "Thanks, Draven. I hope we can help them all."

Congo couldn't help himself. He pressed into Zhaul's touch as much as his muscles would allow . . . for a few seconds, anyway. With a clenched jaw, Congo settled again.

"What's your thoughts, Draven?" Kontra asked.

"They respond to Tim's orders best because he's a warlock," Draven stated. "Just as I'm certain they'd respond better to me as well."

Wait. They didn't know that?

Narrowing his eyes just a smidge, Congo racked his brain. *How could they not have known that?*

Except, then it occurred to Congo—these people hadn't procured his sleuth from the witches. He and his people had

14

been in battle, ordered to help some asshole red fox shifter. They'd been defeated by none other than the Four Horsemen of the Apocalypse.

No surprise there.

When Congo had woken, two of his number hadn't been with them, so he assumed they were dead. In truth, he'd been surprised to wake up at all. The horsemen could so easily have done away with every single one of them.

Congo hadn't seen the witches again.

Instead, Congo had been in a room guarded by demons. The Horseman of Death had arrived and touched each of their heads. While Congo could feel a weird, heavy weight settle over his mind, it hadn't hurt.

Eventually, Death had shaken his head before leaving the room. Congo hadn't known how much time had passed before the horseman had returned. They'd been given food and ordered to eat it. They'd been escorted to the woods to do their business.

All in all, Congo and his people had been treated well.

Then they'd been brought to this home, to this group of shifters with a magick-wielder as one of their leaders.

Congo suddenly wished he could ask who they actually were and what they wanted with him.

Unfortunately, Congo couldn't shift unless ordered to, so he couldn't ask.

And now I found my mate.

Just what the hell am I going to do? I can't keep my people safe. How can I save my mate?

"I order you all to spend two hours relaxing as you see fit, then return here."

Snapping his attention back to the deck—and Tim—Congo gaped, even in bear form.

Seriously?

Congo wanted to believe that would work so very badly. After the first few tentative steps, and no pain slashed through him, he made his first semi-free choice in . . . he wasn't certain how long.

Gripping Zhaul's wrist in his mouth ever-so-gently, Congo tugged his mate toward the trees.

To his pleasure, Zhaul didn't resist.

CHAPTER THREE

Zhaul followed his mate's guidance, allowing him to lead him to the trees. His own bear rumbled with pleasure at getting some alone-time with their mate—sort of. After all, the other brown bears were tentatively making their way to the surrounding cypress trees, too.

Upon reaching the edge of the trees, his brown bear released his wrist. He rested his forepaws on the trunk and peered upward. Then he focused back on Zhaul.

His expression appeared expectant.

Zhaul glanced at the branches, and his own bear rumbled in his mind. Smiling, he asked, "Do you want to go climbing?"

The brown bear growled as he rubbed his big head against Zhaul's chest. Then he scratched at the tree trunk.

"Okay." Zhaul grinned as he whipped his shirt over his head. "I haven't been climbing in forever."

After dropping his clothes on the ground where they fell, Zhaul crouched and called to his bear. His body morphed, growing larger. Thick fur sprouted from his pores, and his limbs altered. Sharp claws extended from his fingers and toes, and his jaw lengthened to accommodate his massive teeth.

Zhaul opened his eyes to find his mate watching him with warmth in his deep brown eyes. As soon as he finished, the brown bear returned his feet to the ground. His mate rubbed his head against Zhaul's in greeting, snuffling and rumbling with obvious happiness.

Returning the touches, Zhaul nuzzled over his mate's ear,

then along his neck and shoulder. He grumbled with pleasure, enjoying the petting. After a moment of that, he felt his mate grip his ear and tug lightly, his movements playful.

Grunting, Zhaul tugged free and attempted to do the same to his mate. The other bear was quicker. He slipped away, his eyes alit with his pleasure. Then the brown bear turned and bounded up the tree.

Zhaul followed, climbing swiftly. His claws dug into the bark of the cypress tree, propelling him upward. He followed his mate along first one branch, then another.

Every once in a while, Zhaul drew close enough to take a playful swipe at his mate's body or a nip at his haunch. On a particularly wide set of branches where it broke into three smaller ones, his brown bear turned and pounced.

Going with the movement, Zhaul rolled backward, his body cradled in the vee the branches had made. His mate landed on top of him, holding him down with his front paws. He immediately began grooming Zhaul, licking his face, ears, and neck.

Zhaul stayed still under his mate's ministrations, allowing his bear to push his head this way and that. After several minutes, the brown bear relaxed against him, and his nose pressed into his neck. Zhaul nuzzled his cheek against the brown bear's, wishing for all he was worth that he could talk to him.

Recalling Tim's words — giving the bears permission to relax as they saw fit — an idea formed.

Calling to his human form, Zhaul changed back. He ignored the scrape of bark on his backside as his shift worked through him. Once he had human limbs, Zhaul reached up and sank his fingers into his mate's fur, enjoying the feel of the coarse hair under his palms.

Zhaul met the bear's brown eyes, seeing the intelligence within their depths. His mate was in there. He knew it.

I just need to get him to come out.

"Can you shift?" Zhaul asked. When the bear just stared at him, he tried again. "Do you have the ability to shift?" After a second of hesitation, Zhaul added, "Or did the witches trap you in your bear form?"

For a moment, Zhaul just waited to see what his mate would decide to try to share with him. He massaged the ruff under his fingers while moving his other hand to rub the fur on his cheek. Smiling at the way his bear pressed into his touches, Zhaul wondered if the bear would try to respond at all.

Finally, the bear dipped his head in a semblance of a nod.

Zhaul realized that could have been an affirmative to any of his questions.

Damn. I didn't think this through.

After a second of hesitation, Zhaul stated, "Tim ordered you to relax as you saw fit." He watched his mate's jaw tightened as he growled softly in agitation. Zhaul decided to press the matter by saying, "That means, if you decided you wanted to relax in human form, you could."

To Zhaul's pleasure, his mate cocked his head. He seemed to be considering that. The bear even swallowed thickly, as if gearing himself up for something.

Then the bear shifted. The transition was slow, and the twisted expression on his features betrayed his agony. The fur beneath Zhaul's figures was replaced by sweaty flesh.

It took nearly two minutes, but finally, his naked human mate lay heavily upon him. He panted harshly, and every few seconds, shudders racked him.

Zhaul recalled the first time he'd managed to shift to his human form after being trapped for almost six months. It had been uncomfortable as hell. His skin had felt on fire, and his joints had ached.

From how his mate was acting, Zhaul wondered if the man had been stuck as a bear for even longer.

Doing his best to soothe, Zhaul rubbed up and down his

mate's back. He enjoyed the feel of his hard muscles under his deep brown flesh. His ribs were a bit more prominent than they should be, telling Zhaul that he needed more than a few good meals.

Gotta remember to mention that to Kontra.

His mate needed more food.

Pressing a kiss to his mate's shaggy, dark-brown hair, Zhaul inhaled his woodsy masculine scent. Even tinged with the acrid bite of pain, he still smelled fantastic. That, coupled with their naked flesh pressed together, had a predictable reaction on Zhaul's body, and he felt his blood heat as his cock stirred.

His mate inhaled deeply and groaned softly. He slid his arms around Zhaul, tightening his hold. Rubbing his cheek against Zhaul's pectoral, his mate also shifted his hips, revealing that he was quickly coming to be in an answering state of need.

Zhaul's instincts reared up, flooding him with an undeniable desire to care for and please his mate. Lowering his hands to his soon-to-be lover's slim hips, he shifted him a little to the left, allowing Zhaul to spread his legs. As soon as Zhaul cradled his mate between his thighs, the feel of the other man's thick erection pressing against his own caused a zing of pleasure to streak up his spine.

"Fuck," Zhaul whined, holding his mate's hips tighter as he rocked his hips. "Tell me this is okay, my mate," he urged, dipping his head to press wet kisses across his temple. "Can I please us both?"

Even as Zhaul asked for permission, he couldn't stop the movement of his hips. It had been so damn long, and the feel of his mate in his arms caused his blood to rage with lust. The heady scent of his mate's arousal set his mouth watering with a desire to taste . . . everything.

"Yessss," his mate hissed, his voice gruff and low, guttural, as if he hadn't used it in a very long time. He tightened his

arms where they were wrapped around Zhaul's torso and began rocking his hips more firmly. "Yessss, maaaate."

His words were slurred and rough, but Zhaul understood.
Having confirmed his mate's acceptance, he sped up his
movements. He knew it wouldn't be long, for he already felt
the tell-tale tingle at the base of his spine and enjoyed the way
his balls began to tighten.

Zhaul slid his palms from his mate's hips to his ass cheeks.
While he felt his lover's body tense a little, he never stopped
moving. Flexing his muscles, Zhaul used the better hold to
increase the pressure.

That seemed to be all his lover needed.

With a gruff moan, his mate was taken by racking shudders to his body. The heat of cum oozing between them, along
with the delicious aroma of his mate's seed, caused Zhaul's
senses to sing. His cock throbbed as his orgasm crashed over
him, sending him soaring.

For several long moments, Zhaul just reveled in the sweet
sensations of holding and marking his mate with his scent.
While his mouth watered with his craving to taste his lover's
blood, he stayed the impulse . . . for now.

Zhaul felt his mate shift above him, easing up his body a
little. Then his lover once again buried his face in Zhaul's
neck. He smiled as he released his man's ass and rubbed up
his back, pleased his mate would find comfort from his scent.

When his mate began to lift his head, Zhaul thought he
would finally get to meet his lover's gaze. Except, he didn't.
His mate stopped with his nose still touching the flesh where
his neck met his shoulder.

"Biiiite meeee," his mate snarled right before sinking his
teeth deep into Zhaul's flesh.

Gasping in shock, Zhaul tensed upon feeling the initial
spike of pain. Then he moaned as the sweetest zings of bliss
fired through his veins. His nipples beaded, and his cock

throbbed.

Zhaul found himself blind-sided by a second orgasm, his balls feeling as if they damn well turned inside out as he coated his mate with another heavy load of jizz.

As his mate continued to suck at Zhaul's neck, his orgasm seemed to go on and on. His brain stalled, and his instinct to bite returned in full force, his canines extending.

Unable to help himself, Zhaul did exactly as his mate had demanded — he bit him.

Snapping his head forward, Zhaul buried his teeth into the flesh where his mate's neck met his shoulder. The other shifter's life force welled up around his teeth, flowing into his mouth. The exquisite flavor of his lover's blood coated his tongue, drawing a deep, satisfied groan from Zhaul's throat.

Zhaul swallowed once, twice, then a third time. The groan and shudder from the man atop him sent a possessive thrill through him, and he clung to his mate even tighter.

Finally, Zhaul gathered a bit of self-control and eased his teeth from his mate's neck. He licked the abused flesh, closing the wound and cleaning away the last traces of delicious fluid all at the same time. Seeing the claiming scar he'd left behind, pride raced through him.

While one of them would have to fuck the other to truly complete their bond, he still loved that he'd left his mark on his mate.

Feeling his mate's arms loosen just a little, Zhaul rubbed over his back once more. He felt the other man ease his teeth free, and the tingles caused by him licking over his mark caused him to hum with pleasure. His dick even twitched, threatening to rise again.

After what felt like an eternity, but was probably really only a few seconds, his mate finally lifted his head.

Zhaul peered into deep, dark, and troubled brown eyes. His mate's shaggy brows were drawn together, and there was a pinch to his bearded lips that worried him.

"I claimed you," the man stated in his deep rough voice. He grimaced as he shook his head. "I shouldn't have done that."

Frowning as his heart began hammering in his chest for an all new reason, Zhaul countered, "It's never wrong to claim your mate."

"But I'm a slave. I have nothing to offer you. I can't even control my own actions."

Shaking his head, Zhaul declared, "You're not a slave. Not anymore, and we'll find a way to break the spells' hold on your actions." Seeing the disbelief etched across his lover's features, he added, "I promise."

CHAPTER FOUR

Congo wanted to believe Zhaul so damn badly. Except, there were warlocks in the group. Had Zhaul been bespelled to believe that he was free?

"I can scent that you don't believe me." Zhaul smiled at him as he teased the fingertips of one hand along Congo's eyebrow, then down his face. "You will . . . in time." Then a wry smile curved Zhaul's lips. "So, uh, what's your name?"

"Congo," he replied, tipping his head into Zhaul's touch. "And you're Zhaul. I heard them call you that."

"Yes," Zhaul confirmed. "How long were you trapped by the witches?"

Shrugging, Congo admitted, "I have no idea. What year is it?"

After hearing Zhaul's answer, Congo couldn't help but blanch. "Uh, damn. They captured us a little over two-and-a-half years ago." He sighed as he rested his forehead against his mate's chest. "I was alpha of a small, reclusive sleuth in the Catskill Mountains," Congo admitted. "There were only twelve of us, all gay bears that banded together to live off the grid, and now our number is half that."

"I'm so sorry," Zhaul murmured, massaging one shoulder as he threaded his fingers through Congo's hair. "I can't imagine how you must feel, thinking you're responsible when it wasn't really your fault."

Congo lifted his head. "How can it not be?" he countered. "I'm the alpha." With a heavy sigh, he admitted on a whisper, "And it makes me an even bigger bastard to feel so grateful that one of the remaining bears is my younger brother." Then Congo grimaced as he shook his head. "Not that I'd wish this continued existence on anyone."

"And now, it's over," Zhaul insisted. "Kontra's mate and his mentor will figure out how to remove the effects of the spells the witches put on you."

Instead of commenting on that, Congo asked, "How did they capture you?"

Congo watched a pink hue invade Zhaul's cheeks as his attention cut to the left. "Uh, I went to a club, and somehow, someone there knew I was a shifter. The guy I was, um" —he cleared his throat before mumbling—"going to hook up with led me into a trap."

Biting back his jealous growl, Congo did his best to shove the sensation deep, deep down. The fact that Zhaul sprawled under him naked, wearing his mark and covered in his cum, certainly helped. His mate's hands on Zhaul definitely helped, too.

"Well, these military or mercenary guys tranqed me, and I woke up in some scientists' facility." Zhaul's features twisted in obvious discomfort as he must have been thinking about that. "Anyway, I was transferred a couple of times. Then Kontra and his guys rescued me. I was only able to shift back to my human form for the first time yesterday."

"Wait." Confusion filled Congo. "What?"

"Uh . . ." Zhaul appeared just as confused as Congo felt. "What, what?"

"A scientists' facility?" Congo finally unwound one arm from beneath Zhaul and reached toward his mate's hair. He intended to thread his fingers between the man's beautiful oddly streaked hair, but then he saw how dirty his fingers were, so he rested them on his mate's shoulder instead. "Kontra and, and T-Tim . . . they rescued you?"

Zhaul nodded. "Yeah. They're the good guys."

25

"B-But . . . they're warlocks," Congo finished on a whisper.

"Tim and Draven are, yeah," Zhaul confirmed. "But they don't cast spells on shifters." Then he rolled his eyes before smirking wryly. "I guess I have heard a couple of stories where Tim's used a spell on a flying shifter to do reconnaissance . . . and then there were times when a shifter attacked him, and he had to defend himself, but that's totally understandable."

"O-Okay." Congo didn't know what to think of that.

Zhaul lightly tugged on Congo's hair before threading it behind his ear. "So, anyway, they'll help as best they can." He sobered a little as he added, "And I'm sorry about the bears you lost." With his expression earnest, Zhaul repeated, "But that wasn't your fault. That was the fault of that evil circle of witches."

Congo forced an absent nod as he felt a skitter of . . . something . . . travel across his nerve endings. Having felt that sensation enough times over the last couple of years, he sighed deeply.

The spell.

"I have to go," Congo rumbled.

"Go?" Zhaul cocked his head. "Go where?"

"Back to the house," Congo explained as he began easing away from Zhaul. "My two hours are almost up."

"Two hours," Zhaul repeated, confused for a second. Then his eyes widened. "Oh, the way Tim phrased the command."

Congo nodded once. "Yes." Unable to help himself, he dipped close and pressed a kiss to the corner of Zhaul's mouth. "I wish . . . I wish things were different."

Feeling the prickly sensations intensifying, Congo knew he'd run out of time. He began to shift, returning to his bear form. At least the change went swifter and didn't hurt as much.

Soon, Congo shook out his fur and rose to his feet. He saw that Zhaul had returned to his giant panda form, too. After a nuzzle to his mate's black and white head, Congo began hurrying through the trees.

With the way the sparks danced across his flesh, Congo picked up his pace. He hadn't realized he'd traveled so far, and by the time the house came into view between the trees, the tingles had turned to tendrils of fire. When Congo attempted to descend the tree, he lost his balance and flopped gracelessly off the last branch.

Congo grunted in pain, but he forced himself back to his feet. In the next instant, Zhaul's bear was at his side, offering support, nuzzling him encouragingly. Limping with the pain of being late, Congo made his way to his sleuth's side, flopping to the ground when he reached them.

The hyena shifter Congo had seen through the window strolled across the deck. He was eating a blue ice pop while smirking at Congo. Then the male turned his gaze to Zhaul and grinned as he sniffed the air exaggeratedly.

"Damn, Zhaul," the hyena shifter teased. "You must be one hell of a fuck to exhaust this guy so bad that he has to crawl back here." Cackling, he added, "You'll have to share your techniques, man."

"I don't think his movements are caused by exhaustion, Payson," Kontra rumbled from where he sat on the top step. His legs were spread, and Tim was seated before him on the stair below. "That looked like pain."

"Oh, does rutting in bear form hurt?" Payson asked, his brows furrowing. "Never fucked as an animal myself. I wonder if Land would be up for that."

"Land most certainly would *not*," a slender, geeky-looking human countered, exiting the front door. "I love your hyena and all, but just . . . no."

Payson grabbed the human and tugged him close, allowing him to slide the hand not holding his freezie pop up under the guy's shirt. "Okay, baby," he purred into the man's ear.

"We'll leave the bestiality to these guys."

"Uh, we were in human form, and I don't think two shifters mating in their animal form would even be considered bestiality." Zhaul's voice drew Congo's attention. Frowning, he continued, "And we didn't do anything to cause pain." His brows furrowed as he added, "Although, somehow, he knew when his two hours were about up."

"They all did." Tim indicated the others who were once again spread before the warlock. Rubbing the back of his neck, he grumbled, "But how?"

Draven rested on the top step on the other side of the stairs. A dark-haired wolf shifter stood behind him, leaning against the support post. The shifter rested a hand on Draven's shoulder and was rubbing.

"I'm going with the spells woven around these guys causes pain," Draven guessed—astutely. "If they don't obey, pain. If they do something they're not ordered to do, pain." Grimacing, he added, "He was told to be back here in two hours, and he was a minute or two late, so the spells caused pain."

"Well, that fucking sucks," Payson muttered with a scowl. "Fucking witches."

"Shit," Tim mumbled, a distressed expression creasing his features. "I'm sorry. When I said what I did, I didn't mean—" Sighing deeply, Tim peered over his shoulder at Kontra. "You did say we'd have to be careful how we worded things."

"I did," Kontra confirmed as he threaded his fingers through Tim's sandy-blond hair in what looked to be a soothing manner. "But we don't know what those witches did so we're bound to fuck up here and there." Turning his attention to Zhaul, Kontra asked, "You said you shifted? Both of you? To human form?"

Zhaul nodded. "They can shift, although from how Congo did it, my guess is they were trapped longer than my own six months." Kneeling beside Congo, he rubbed at the fur behind his ear. "You doing okay now?"

Congo blinked once, wishing he could reassure his mate. Unfortunately, he hadn't been ordered to answer or to move.

Turning back to those on the porch, Zhaul revealed, "His sleuth was kidnapped from somewhere in the Catskills. They were a small group. A dozen of them." He furrowed his brows as he softly added, "Now their numbers are halved, and he feels responsible."

As the few things that Congo had told Zhaul poured out of his mate's mouth, unease slithered up his spine. He knew his mate trusted these people, but he didn't. Congo had never met any paranormal group that coexisted with magick and shifters equally.

One had always controlled the other.

Unable to help himself, Congo grumbled as worry flooded him.

"Hey, it's okay," Zhaul soothed. He rubbed over Congo's head, having obviously scented his distress. "I told you. These are the good guys." Turning a pleading focus on Kontra and the warlocks, Zhaul added, "You can fix it, right?"

Draven sighed deeply as he and Tim exchanged a look. When he refocused on Zhaul and Congo, he quietly stated, "Those witches used demon blood in their magick to weave these spells." Shrugging, he added, "Spells I don't even know."

Frowning at Tim, Zhaul countered hotly, "But you said you had a vision. A vision of us together."

Tim nodded, not denying that claim. "I did." A thoughtful expression caused his brows to furrow. "But . . . we need more information."

"Hey," the wolf shifter piped up, tugging at Draven's short, white-blond hair. "Remember when I told you the spell that witch used on me so you could try to figure out the counter-spell?"

Draven smiled up at him. "Of course, my beloved."

Congo started. Between the word beloved and the fangs on clear display in Draven's mouth, he realized something. Draven wasn't just a warlock. He was also a vampire.

Taking a chance, Congo attempted to shift. Pain ignited in his blood. Fiery agony coursed through his limbs.

Still, he continued to try.

"I order you to shift."

Congo barely heard Draven's shouted order over the sounds of roaring. Immediately, the agony subsided. Panting hard, Congo snapped his mouth shut, and the sound ceased.

Once back in human form, Congo breathed deeply, doing his best to gain control of himself . . . and find his voice. The feel of Zhaul's hands rubbing his back soothed him. Turning his head a little, Congo did his best to peer up at him, offering him an appreciative smile.

Draven crouched before him, his blue eyes holding a wealth of concern. "You have something to say."

That wasn't an order, so Congo continued to stare. There was only so much pain he could endure at a time.

Grimacing, Draven shook his head. "Let me see if I can get this right," he muttered, obviously thinking. After a glance over his shoulder at the others, Draven peered around at the group. "I order you all to speak freely whenever you feel the need." After another heartbeat, the vampire added, "And I order you to use whichever form you feel necessary, whenever you wish."

Draven hesitated again before saying, "And I order you to only follow orders if they come from Kontra. Otherwise, the choice to follow orders is yours."

Congo felt something loosen in his chest. He cut his gaze from Draven to Tim and finally to Kontra. The grizzly shifter didn't exactly appear pleased, but he didn't seem upset, either.

Obviously reading Kontra's expression, Draven shrugged. "Freeing them to make choices should be a start until we can get those damn spells under control." He pointed. "And you're the alpha."

Kontra sighed deeply even as he nodded once. "I just hate the responsibility of their free will being reliant on my words."

"It's better than nothing."

Whipping his attention to the left upon hearing Madagascar's voice for the first time in years, Congo grinned. "Right you are, brother," he muttered. "Right you are."

Now, gods willing, Zhaul's faith in these men is not misplaced.

CHAPTER FIVE

Zhaul watched as some of Congo's tension seemed to ease from his frame. His smile as he peered at the other burly, dark-haired male caused a sliver of jealousy to stab through his gut. Then Congo's words registered.

Brother. That's his brother.

Well, that's good. Otherwise, I would have had to kick the dude's ass.

Pushing the uncharitable thoughts to the side, Zhaul watched as Congo seemed focused on all the bear shifters. Other than his brother, they were each slowly finishing up a long and painful-sounding shift. Congo's concern for each and every one of them was clear on his features.

"Why the hell would you put yourself through that to try to shift?" Congo's brother asked, frowning at the man. "You knew what would happen." Then the guy's attention shifted to Draven. "Thank you for catching on, by the way, vampire."

Draven dipped his chin in a nod. "I'm sorry you all have been be-spelled in such a way." He focused on Congo. "You are the alpha?"

Congo nodded. "I am. Congo." He tapped his own chest. Then he pointed around the group. "My brother, Madagascar. Cousin, Valentine. Those are friends, Shannon, Zion, and Eurik."

"Good to finally meet you all," Kontra stated, not bothering to rise. "This is my mate, Tim." He pointed toward those on the deck. "That's one of my enforcers, Payson, and his mate, Land. Also, Draven's mate, Vail." Then his eyes narrowed. "If you're homophobes, we'll find another place for you to recover."

"That would be counterproductive," Madagascar rumbled with a snort. His bushy-bearded lips curved into a smirk as he waved between them all. "We're all gay."

Zion lifted his hand. "Bisexual, but labels suck, so who gives a shit."

"Well said." A very tall, slender male rounded the corner. "I'm Doctor Eli Raetz, and I'll be checking you out now that you're all in human form."

"Checking us out, Doc?" Shannon waggled his brows. "I've always had a love for role-play, but this'll be even better."

A low growl came from the small, black male who followed Eli.

Smirking, Eli indicated him, saying, "This is my mate, Sam Bailey."

"Damn." Shannon sounded so damn disappointed. "Sorry, Sam." He lifted his hands in placation. "I haven't gotten laid in . . ." Shannon paused and frowned, his attention turning to Congo. "How long have we been stuck like this?"

Congo frowned as he rubbed the back of his neck. "Two and a half years."

Eurik groaned as he rubbed his hands over his face. "Fuck me. Seriously?"

"Afraid so," Congo confirmed. Then his countenance sobered, and he focused on Zion. "I am so damn sorry about your cousin."

Zion heaved a sigh as his gaze fell to the ground. "It's not your fault." When he lifted his focus to Congo, there was obvious pain in his gaze, but there was no accusation. "There wasn't a damn thing you" — scoffing, he rolled his eyes — "hell, not a damn thing *any* of us could do." Growling, Zion added, "It's all on those fucking witches." He focused on Kontra. "Are any of those bitches still alive? I'd really like to tear the throat out of one or two of them."

Upon his declaration, several others of the bears all snarled their agreement.

Kontra lifted one hand in placation while keeping his other on Tim's shoulder. "I'm sorry. I have absolutely no idea. I'll ask Famine when he brings the other shifters to us."

"What would you like to ask me?"

Zhaul gaped as Famine appeared . . . with a whole bunch of others in tow.

Famine spotted the bears and smiled. "Ah, you got them to shift."

"Holy shit," Madagascar cried. "What the hell? How'd he just appear like that?" Then he scrambled back a little, crab-walking. "Is he a warlock, too?"

"Easy, brother," Congo rumbled, even as he put himself between Madagascar and Famine.

"Relax. Settle down," Kontra called, rising swiftly and putting himself between Famine, his group, and the bears. "This is Famine, one of the Four Horsemen," he explained. "He's just bringing some more shifters for us to look after." Then he frowned. "At this rate, I'm going to need another doctor." Swinging around, Kontra called, "Payson, find Yuma and Hunter. We're going to need another couple pairs of hands."

When Kontra turned, he scowled as he swept his gaze over the six naked bear shifters sprawled on the lawn.

That was when Zhaul noticed it, too. While all of them were reclining as if relaxing, all six screamed of anxiety. Their features were tense, and they breathed heavily.

What the hell?

Zhaul gripped Congo's hand, massaging lightly. "What is it?" he asked, concerned. "Are you hurt?"

Sweat beaded on Congo's brow. He opened his mouth, then closed it again. His dark eyes darted around the clearing, which was quickly filling up with people.

"Oh, for fucks sake," Kontra bellowed, resting his hands on his hips. "This is why I didn't want that power, Draven."

The vampire-warlock lifted his hands. "I'm sorry."

Glancing around the group, Zhaul demanded, "What's that mean? What's going on?" He frowned as he continued to watch his lover lie sprawled on the grass as if ready for a nap. "What did you do?"

Kontra let out a growling sigh. "I told them to relax, remember?" Rubbing a hand over his goateed face, he mumbled, "Gotta watch my damn words." He lowered his hand and focused on the men. "I rescind my order to calm down and relax."

"Oh, damn," Madagascar mumbled, flopping back to stare at the sky. "That was . . . weird."

Zhaul was quickly coming to realize that, given free will, Congo's brother was the dramatic one.

Even as the others nodded a bit and glanced between them, Zhaul squeezed Congo's hand. "Are you okay?"

Congo swallowed hard, forcing a tight smile. "Yeah. Uh, I was going to say I'll be fine." Then he frowned. "But I don't know if that's true." Then Congo flashed what might have been a reassuring smile Zhaul's way before focusing on Draven. "Uh, you're at least part vampire, right?" Congo tapped his teeth. "Fangs."

Draven nodded as he began passing out blankets, which the newly arrived Yuma and Hunter had brought. "I am." With a smarmy smile, he added, "But don't worry. I'm mated. I won't try to bite you or yours."

"Not where I was going with my question . . . or why I tried so hard to shift without command," Congo admitted while rubbing his thumb over the back of Zhaul's hand, perhaps needing it to soothe him. When Congo spoke next, Zhaul understood why. "I had a vampire friend for a couple of decades, before he had to switch covens due to lack of aging. When he tranced someone for blood, he could look into their memories." After another second of hesitation, Congo pressed, "Can you do that?"

Draven's eyes narrowed, his expression turning serious. "Yes. I can do that."

"Brother, don't," Madagascar whispered, clutching his blanket to his chest. "Don't do that."

Congo met his brother's worried—hell, pained—expression. His lips turning into a grim line, he murmured, "His beloved said he needed to know the spell in order to figure out a counter-spell. If he's willing to see, to hear and experience, and can then fix us, I'm willing to relive the memories."

Madagascar's jaw clenched, and his nostrils flared. After a sharp shake of his head, he rumbled, "Nothing I say will persuade you?"

With his smile appearing to turn caring, Congo glanced around at what was left of his sleuth. "No." He refocused on his brother. "The alpha cares for his sleuth. I need to do this."

"What are you talking about?" Zhaul cut in. He could scent Madagascar's sadness and frustration but also Congo's resolve. "What memories are you talking about?"

"Yes," Draven cut in. "What memories *are* you talking about?"

Congo smiled at Zhaul, tight lines around the corners of his lips. Turning his attention to Draven, he explained, "When the witches were casting their spells, they were cutting sigils into our backs." His jaw clenched as he whispered, "Four of us were all strapped over stone altars at a time, and I was in a position to see what was carved into Madagascar's back." Meeting Draven's gaze, he revealed, "I can show you not only what was chanted, but what was cut into our skin." Grimacing, he added, "We're shifters, so we healed fast. We don't have scars."

Zhaul didn't like the shudder that worked through his mate.

With his voice strained, Congo whispered, "While there are no visible marks, the power of the sigil still remains, and we are bound by it."

"Oh, gods, Congo," Zhaul whispered, wrapping his other arm around his mate's torso. Although the words seemed so inadequate, he whispered, "I'm so sorry."

Suddenly, being experimented on by scientists didn't seem so bad. While sure, at times it hurt like hell, he hadn't been forced to do things against his will.

Congo turned and pressed his face against Zhaul's neck. Inhaling noisily, he revealed he was taking comfort from his mate's scent. Zhaul held him tightly, offering what little comfort he could.

"You know, I think Death or War might still have a couple of those witches alive in their realm." Famine appeared a few feet away, and Zhaul turned his head to eye him. When Congo did the same and angry growls sounded from several of the other bear shifters, Famine curved his lips into a cruel smile. "From what I understand about this plane's paranormal restitution, since they put you in situations where members of your sleuth ended up killed, their lives are forfeit." His cold smile widened. "And the honor of their demise would be in your hands."

Hearing Congo's angry growl mixed with the others of his be-spelled sleuth, Zhaul barely refrained from joining in. Those bitches had hurt his mate. They deserved everything coming to them.

Famine chuckled coldly. "Well, I'll contact my brothers and see what can be arranged." Then he dipped his head in a nod and turned away. As Famine moved toward the edge of the property, he called to Kontra, "Thank you, Alpha. I appreciate your assistance."

Then the horseman disappeared, as did his demons.

With the clearing partially cleared out, Zhaul gaped at who remained behind. Just as Famine had claimed, he'd brought an elephant, a camel, a capybara, a gray wolf, and . . . well, Zhaul assumed there was a coral snake around there somewhere. Several of Kontra's people walked among them, talking softly, probably asking yes or no questions, just as they'd once done for Zhaul.

"If you're willing to relive the memories," Draven rumbled softly, drawing Zhaul's attention to where the vampire focused on Congo. "I will experience them with you."

"Are you certain?" Congo clarified, his dark brows furrowed. "They are not . . . pretty."

Draven scoffed softly, his expression understanding. "I bet not, but they are yours, and they could help your people." His blue eyes glimmered in the afternoon sunlight. "I know that's what you want the most, and I'm more than willing to do my part to help."

Congo nodded once. "Thank you."

Madagascar reached over and gripped Congo's wrist.

Zhaul could read the love in the brothers' eyes as they exchanged a poignant look.

Then it passed, Madagascar focused on Sam and his questions about his health, and Congo returned his attention to Draven.

The vampire nodded once, then rose to his feet. "Let's go somewhere secluded where we can get comfortable."

Helping Congo to his feet, Zhaul refused to leave his mate's side . . . no matter what happened.

CHAPTER SIX

Resting his forearms on the shower wall, Congo pressed his head to the cool stone between them. He stood still, relishing the feel of the hot water cascading over him. His mind still played flashes of his memories behind his eyelids, and he struggled to put everything into perspective.

Free. Well, as free as I can be until these blasted spells are broken.

Just as Madagascar had said. *Better than nothing.*

Feeling Zhaul's hands land on his back, Congo jolted.

"Easy, my mate," Zhaul crooned into his ear. "Just taking care of you."

Congo would have countered—he couldn't remember the last time he hadn't been the one caring for someone else—but Zhaul's soapy fingers massaging his tense back felt too damn good. Plus, they helped to banish his memories, giving him something else to focus on.

My mate.

After years of torture, Fate had blessed Congo with a mate—someone to give him a reason to combat the darkness of his dreams, the guilt of his memories. He knew Zhaul had faced his own trials in order to stand beside him, and he hated that, but life had a way of circling around.

Feeling Zhaul dig his fingertips into a particularly tight muscle, Congo groaned and arched. He hissed and pushed into the touch. His mate didn't disappoint, working the tender area until his tension eased.

"There you go, my mate," Zhaul rumbled, pressing a kiss to his nape. "We'll get you all relaxed before I take you to bed and fuck you."

Congo barked a laugh and peered over his shoulder at the other bear shifter. His mate was almost as big as him, maybe an inch shy of his own six-foot-four height. His shoulders were wide, and his body strong.

What would being pounded by this man feel like?

"Never done that before," Congo admitted, meeting Zhaul's gaze. That was when he spotted the teasing light in his mate's eyes. "Zhaul?"

Grinning, Zhaul leaned forward and pecked a kiss to Congo's cheek. "I guessed that." Then he rolled his eyes. "Or if you had, it'd been a really, *really* long time ago." Waggling his eyebrows, Zhaul purred huskily. "You're in luck. I'm a switch." Then his eyes narrowed. "I'll have your ass someday, but tonight, I think you need to be in mine."

Congo's breath caught in his throat. His cock went from flaccid to throbbing in less than a second. The reallocation of blood nearly caused him to swoon, and he knew it was a damn good thing he'd been leaning against the wall or he would have embarrassed himself.

As it was, Congo could think of little else than getting to the bed in the adjoining room as swiftly as possible.

"Relax, my mate," Zhaul rumbled into his ear, nuzzling his cheek against Congo's neck to push his long, wet hair out of the way. Before Zhaul began nibbling down his neck, he crooned, "We'll get to that very soon. First, let me make you more comfortable." His mate nipped at his earlobe before whispering, "I know how much I adored my first hot shower after months without. Let me give this to you."

Sighing, Congo nodded. "Thank you."

Zhaul's words reminded him that his mate understood. As much as their need perfumed the air, his panda shifter would never begrudge him the simple joy of a shower. Instead, Zhaul made it an even more euphoric experience.

Congo pressed into each massaging touch, which caused

goose bumps to break out on his skin. His lover's strong fingers soothed away knots that had been there . . . forever. The heat of his palms was nothing compared to the scrape of his nails, spreading tingles over every nerve ending.

Delicious. Sensual. Mind-blowing.

By the time Zhaul had finished cleaning Congo from top to bottom — including washing and conditioning his hair, twice — Congo felt like a puddle of goo. Well, other than his aching cock. His erection twitched in time with his heartbeat, and Congo's mouth watered for another taste of Zhaul's beyond incredible blood.

Except, when Zhaul turned off the water and urged him from the shower, he didn't lead him straight to the bed. He wrapped a towel around him, drying him in slow, sensual strokes. Then Zhaul guided him to the sink where he handed over a toothbrush covered in toothpaste.

"Brush," Zhaul urged softly. "While I set up."

Confused, Congo asked, "Set up?"

Zhaul nodded as he turned on the hot water. "It'll just take a minute."

While still confused — and hornier than hell — Congo did as his mate bid. He brushed his teeth — which, really, he knew was a good idea. As he cleaned his mouth for the first time in years, he anticipated kissing his mate.

Of course he wants me to brush.

Once Congo finished, he set the brush aside. He cupped his hands under the water and splashed it over his mouth. Doing that twice more, he cleared away all traces of paste from his beard. As Congo patted dry his way-too-bushy whiskers, he glanced around for a razor but didn't see one.

Making a mental note to ask for one later, Congo headed out of the bathroom. He stopped, surprise filling him — and . . . gratefulness.

Zhaul had placed what appeared to be a rolling office chair on top of several spread-out towels. On the nearby dresser, he'd laid out a number of items—a pair of scissors, a pot of cream, a straight razor, a bowl of water, and a couple of piles of towels.

Smiling, Zhaul encouraged, "Have a seat."

It seemed his mate wasn't done pampering him.

Crossing to the chair, Congo settled in it, grateful for the towel Zhaul had thoughtfully draped over it, since his ass was still bare. He felt Zhaul lower the chair, obviously adjusting him to the height he wanted. Then his mate hurried around and lifted his feet onto a low stool, causing Congo to tip back in the chair.

Once Zhaul seemed to have Congo situated the way he wanted him, he grabbed another towel and draped it around his chest and shoulders. Standing over him, he held up the pair of scissors. "How short do you usually keep it?" he asked, eyeing his beard. Meeting his gaze, he added, "Or do you normally go clean-shaven?"

Congo smiled up at Zhaul. "I haven't gone clean-shaven since I was sixteen," he admitted with a chuckle. "Of course, that was back in eighteen-twenty, so . . ." With a wink, Congo told him, "Just a little longer than yours."

While Congo loved the feel of Zhaul's closely shorn, barely-there beard rubbing against his cheeks and lips, he preferred a bit more length on his cheeks.

"Sculpted or not?" Zhaul questioned as he began snipping the too-long hairs around Congo's cheeks. His fingers gently pushed Congo's head this way and that.

Relaxing under his mate's ministrations, Congo murmured, "I'll let you decide, my mate. Do what you want with me."

Congo couldn't remember the last time he hadn't shaved himself, and the novel experience—plus the fact that it was his mate who'd thought to take such fantastic care of him—felt like the best kind of pampering.

"Okay, with your dark skin and strong jawline, I'm going to go with lightly sculpted," Zhaul told him, his voice coming out just as soft.

Then no words were needed.

When Zhaul was finished with the scissors, he rubbed cream around the edges of Congo's face, urging him to tip his head back. Allowing his eyes to slide shut, Congo put his faith in his mate as the other man began sliding the blade across his flesh. As Zhaul slid the sharp edge along the skin of Congo's neck, he petted him lightly, as if to soothe, to reassure.

But Congo had absolute faith in the shifter Fate had chosen for him. His mate's hand wouldn't slip. Even if it did, one lick and the nick would be sealed by his mate's saliva.

Hell, that might even feel good. After all, biting sure does.

Congo smiled at his thoughts, and Zhaul cautioned him. "Stay still, my mate," he whispered, rubbing his thumb over Congo's Adam's apple. Just as quietly, he lifted the blade and asked, "What has you smiling so?"

Smiling wider, Congo cracked an eyelid open and peered up at Zhaul. "Feels good," he told him softly. "Thank you for taking care of me."

Congo couldn't remember the last time he'd felt so . . . cared for.

Zhaul smiled back down at him. "It's my pleasure." Dipping his head, Zhaul pressed a chaste kiss to his lips before straightening and returning to his shaving.

Sighing, Congo allowed his eyelid to slip closed again and reveled in the exquisite sensation of his mate's gentle hands on him.

When Zhaul finally wiped Congo's face and told him, "There. Finished," he'd damn near fallen asleep.

Of course, that didn't mean his erection had softened one iota. Not even feeling the blade at his throat had deflated him. Instead, Congo's need had only built, despite the alternate kind of bliss Zhaul had offered him.

Congo opened his eyes to see Zhaul smiling uncertainly at him. *Huh?* Zhaul was also holding up a mirror. *Oh, of course.*

Realizing Zhaul worried about what Congo would think about his shaving job, he peered at his reflection, ready to offer his mate's reassurances. His words stuck in his throat.

When Congo had been in the bathroom, he hadn't taken a real good look at himself. Once he'd spotted the slightly tired, haunted look in his eyes and the bushy beard, he hadn't cared to look further. Now, however, while there were still fatigue-lines around his eyes, Congo saw affection in his eyes, instead. Zhaul's attentions had done that, given him a sense of peace.

The expertly trimmed beard was just the icing on the cake.

Snapping his focus back to Zhaul, Congo rose to his feet. He saw his mate shift from foot to foot, clearly worried. Deciding that wouldn't do at all, Congo cradled Zhaul's cheeks between his palms.

"Damn, babe," Congo rumbled. "You're amazing."

Then Congo sealed his lips over Zhaul's and took the kiss he so desperately wanted. He thrust his tongue past his mate's lips, demanding entrance. His mate didn't seem to mind, for he opened instantly.

Congo slid one hand to Zhaul's nape, threading his fingers through his still-wet hair. He lowered his other arm to band it around his mate's waist. Taking the kiss deep, Congo explored his lover as he brought his mate's body flush against his own.

Feeling the towel between them, the one Zhaul had wrapped around his own waist at some point, Congo decided it had to go. As he slid his tongue against Zhaul's, he gripped the towel's edge and tugged, freeing it. He mapped Zhaul's mouth in slow, languorous licks while dropping the offending fabric to the floor.

When Congo returned his palm to Zhaul's backside, he

landed it on his mate's ass. He squeezed the firm round flesh and tightened his hold again, causing their naked bodies to press together from knees to shoulders. He felt Zhaul's hands on his back, telling him his mate had set the mirror down at some point, but he didn't care when or where.

Instead, as Congo ate at Zhaul's mouth and rocked his hips, rutting against his mate's answering thickness, all he cared about was the man in his arms and how he wanted to return the pleasure his mate had given him.

Breaking the kiss, Congo sucked in a ragged breath. He stared at Zhaul, carnal hunger surging through him upon seeing his mate's flushed cheeks, kiss-swollen lips, and heavy-lidded eyes.

"You're gorgeous," Congo rumbled gruffly. "And I want you. I want to make you mine."

Be-spelled or not, Congo couldn't resist taking what Fate had deemed his, and Zhaul was all his.

Relief surged through Congo when Zhaul gasped, "Yes. Gods, yes. I'm yours."

"Mine."

Then Congo gripped Zhaul's hips, lifted his mate, and tossed him to the middle of the bed.

CHAPTER SEVEN

Zhaul stared up at Congo, surprise and anticipation thrumming through him in equal measure. Sharing his psyche with a giant panda bear, Zhaul was a pretty big guy with more than a little extra around the middle. He'd never been with anyone who could toss him around like that.

Of course, he'd never been with a shifter, either.

He found it arousing as hell. His cock throbbed as he watched Congo prowl onto the bed. Spotting the thick shaft jutting from his mate's groin, his chute muscles clenched, but not from fear.

Anticipation screamed through Zhaul. He wanted his mate just as badly as Congo appeared to want him. The hunger burning in his lover's dark eyes consumed every possible doubt.

"Love the way you're looking at me," Congo rumbled, his heated gaze narrowing. His lips curved into a sensuous smile as he rested his palms on Zhaul's thighs. "Want to see what other expressions you make."

When Zhaul felt Congo's palms slide up the inside of his sensitive skin, the need in his gut intensified. Heat surged through his veins. In response to the pressure Congo applied to his inner thighs, Zhaul spread his legs wider, offering his mate more room.

"Where's your lube, Zhaul?" Congo asked, teasing his thumbs through his pubic hair.

The tingles spreading through Zhaul's groin from the teasing massage made finding his tongue difficult. Flailing one hand, he glanced toward the nightstand. Once he'd shifted, he'd been given a room in the old Victorian to recover. The gang had also supplied him with everything he could possibly want to see to his needs, including lube.

Congo levered to the side, reaching over to open the drawer and fish inside.

Unable to help himself, Zhaul reached up and rubbed his fingers over the side of Congo's strong frame. He teased along his ribcage and over the delineated lines of his abdominals. When Congo drew back, he rested his weight on one elbow, so Zhaul moved his fingers to his chest, teasing around one nipple.

Congo groaned softly under Zhaul's touch, drawing his gaze back to his face. His mate smiled as he watched Zhaul's hand smoothing over him.

"Your tanned hand looks absolutely amazing against my dark flesh," Congo rumbled before meeting Zhaul's gaze. He waggled the bottle of lube he held. "Not open."

Zhaul shrugged, feeling his cheeks heat a little. "Hadn't yet felt the urge to jack off."

Humming, Congo quickly opened the bottle. "Well, when you do." He pinned Zhaul with a feral look. "I want to watch."

Sucking in a sharp breath, Zhaul stared at Congo in surprise. "Y-You do?"

Congo nodded once, very slowly. "Oh, yes. I would love to see you play with your gorgeous cock." He lowered his attention to Zhaul's dick. "To learn how you like to be touched." Pouring lube onto his palm, Congo added, "To know what pleases you most."

Then Congo wrapped his greased palm around Zhaul's erection and stroked in long, leisurely strokes—top to bottom and back again, swiping over his crown in the process.

Zhaul shuddered, staring, as he watched Congo fondle

him. Sparks of dark pleasure coiled in his gut. Panting harshly, he felt his balls begin to tighten just from Congo levering over him and stroking his dick.

Maybe it was because he hadn't had another man's hand on his dick in over a year. Maybe it was because this was his mate. Either way, Zhaul felt himself riding the brink embarrassingly fast.

That didn't stop him from wanting what Congo was so freely giving him.

"Oh, yessss," Congo hissed, his dark eyes full of knowing. "You're right there, aren't you, baby?"

Snapping his gaze to Congo's face, Zhaul saw the smug satisfaction filling his countenance. Unable — and unwilling — to lie to his mate, Zhaul jerked a nod. "Yeah."

Congo slid his wet hand down and cupped Zhaul's balls, squeezing and rolling experimentally.

Moaning, Zhaul spread his legs wider, offering more room, begging with his body for more. "O-Oh!" His testicles had always been sensitive, and for his mate to play with them without asking caused a squirt of pre-ejaculate to erupt from his dick.

"Damn, you're sensitive," Congo purred, sounding pleased as hell. "Could I get you off just like this, Zhaul?"

"Y-Yeah," Zhaul managed to say, because it was the truth. He'd done it to himself many times, but this was his mate, whose touch was ten times better than his own.

"I want to see that," Congo claimed, and his actions confirmed his words. He continued to gently roll Zhaul's testicles, only to pause and squeeze them in a few rhythmic pumps before rolling them again. "I want to see your balls pull up and pour your seed all over your chest."

Zhaul whined and shuddered. His cock leaked like a sieve, spilling seed over the side of his head to pool on his stomach. He was so close, but he couldn't find his voice to tell Congo that. The stimulation to his nuts took his breath away.

"What would happen if I licked them, Zhaul?" Congo asked softly, gruffly. "Drew them into my mouth and sucked?"

Just the image was all Zhaul needed to fly over that precipice. With a shout of Congo's name, he was there, soaring, watching his mate watch him as he poured his life essence all over himself in great bliss-inducing gouts. With Congo still teasing his testicles, Zhaul's orgasm went on and on, his senses reeling, his eyes practically rolling to the back of his head as he rode the cloud of endorphins.

When Zhaul finally came back to himself, he noticed two things. First, Congo was crouched over him, licking his spend from his stomach. Second, his mate had at least two fingers in his ass.

"There you are, Zhaul," Congo rumbled, barely pausing in his cleaning. His deep brown eyes practically glowed with pleasure. "That was truly the sexiest fucking thing I've ever seen." His free hand rubbed over Zhaul's hip and up his side. "My sexy mate."

Zhaul moaned as he felt Congo massage his prostate while pressing another finger into him, stretching him wider. "Y-You're the s-sexy one," he managed to counter. "Miles of dark, muscled flesh."

Congo grinned before sticking out his tongue and scooping up a particularly large glob. Then he leaned forward and pressed his lips to Zhaul's. As Congo pushed his tongue into Zhaul's mouth, sharing his seed, Zhaul moaned again, accepting the offering.

Breaking the kiss, Congo murmured, "You taste delicious. Knew you would."

Zhaul watched wide-eyed and panting as Congo returned to his stomach, licked up more, only to come and share it with him again. Having never before tasted himself, Zhaul found his mate's actions sexy and dirty in the most primitive of ways. He also couldn't seem to get enough of it, happy to lick himself off Congo's tongue each time he offered.

Finally, Congo seemed to be satisfied, for he rocked back to his knees. "You're ready, my mate."

Easing his fingers free of Zhaul's body, Congo grabbed a pillow with his clean hand. Congo used his wet hand to grip Zhaul's butt cheek and lift him, allowing him to shove the pillow under him, canting his hips upward.

Zhaul watched as Congo poured more lube onto his jutting erection. At the same time, his mate petted Zhaul's groin, teasing his fingertips around the base of his still-hard dick, then down to use a thumb to tug at the rim of his hole, opening him a little. His mate's focus seemed riveted to the sight of his waiting opening as he leisurely massaged his rod.

Clenching his anal muscles, Zhaul felt a rush of renewed arousal surge through him. His mate had to be eleven inches if he was an inch, and his girth was hefty. Zhaul knew the other bear shifter would split him wide open, and he couldn't wait to feel it, to feel his mate in him, connected in such a primal way. Zhaul needed to feel it so damn badly, his mate fucking and taking him.

"Please," Zhaul whispered, rocking his hips up invitingly. "Need you."

Congo offered him a lazy smile full of heat. "Need me, my mate?" He tugged at Zhaul's opening again before glancing pointedly at his own cock. "Need this?" Rocking his hips a little, Congo stroked himself. "Need my cock in you?"

Zhaul sucked in a harsh breath as he nodded eagerly. "So damn badly."

"Then you'll have me," Congo told him.

As if that had been the permission Congo had been waiting on, he pointed his cock toward Zhaul's opening. He eased forward on his knees a little at a time until his dick head kissed

Zhaul's stretched hole. With a grunt, Congo pushed, popping his wide head past Zhaul's guardian muscle.

The stretch was intense, but the burn was mild, and just what Zhaul needed. "Oh, gods, Congo," he muttered, clamping experimentally on his mate's dick head. "So good."

"Yeeeahhh," Congo rumbled through gritted teeth, his smile appearing feral. "Do that. Milk my knob. Show me how much you want the rest of me in you, buried deep."

Zhaul wouldn't have been able to stop even if he'd wanted to. His anal walls seemed to obey without his control. Over and over, he squeezed his mate's huge cock head.

As Zhaul did that, he watched Congo's chest heave with barely leashed need. His mate stared at where they were joined, a feral smile curving his lips. His nostrils flared, and a bead of sweat dripped down his temple.

After what felt like a damn eternity, Congo finally flipped his attention to Zhaul's face. His eyes seemed to be lit with some inner glow, and he peered at him hungrily. Holding Zhaul's gaze, Congo slid his palms under Zhaul's ass cheeks, gripping one in each hand.

Congo squeezed and lifted, drawing Zhaul toward him, pulling him onto his cock.

Zhaul felt himself slide across the bed as his passage opened, stretching further than he thought possible, as Congo speared him on his dick. Once fully seated—Congo's groin flushed to Zhaul's ass—Congo moved his hands to Zhaul's hips. He pulled him even tighter to his lap, not letting him move, just experiencing the stretch of being seated on Congo's long, thick erection.

Tipping back his head, closing his eyes, Congo let out a long, ragged moan. Ecstasy creased his features, telling Zhaul he was reveling in the sensation of being buried in Zhaul as deeply as he could go. His chest heaved with his harsh breaths.

Mesmerized, Zhaul couldn't tear his gaze away from the blissful expression on Congo's dark features.

Finally, Congo opened his eyes and met his gaze. A warm smile curved his lips. He let out a long, slow breath.

"You feel . . . amazing, my mate," Congo whispered, his voice husky, full of arousal and satisfaction at the same time. Still sporting that same happy smile, Congo lowered his gaze to where he impaled Zhaul. For another few heartbeats, he stared once more. Then he lifted his attention to Zhaul again. This time a bear-like grin spread across his face, showing lots of teeth. "I'm going to be right here" — he rocked his hips a bit to emphasize his point, jostling his dick in Zhaul's ass and causing a riot of tingles to erupt through his inner flesh — "a lot."

Panting, the need for Congo to move surging through him, Zhaul whispered, "Gods, yes, please. Anytime."

"My mate."

Then, finally, Congo began to move.

CHAPTER EIGHT

Sighing heavily, Congo nuzzled the back of Zhaul's neck. He couldn't believe how swiftly his life had changed—again. Just that morning, he thought he was a prisoner of a pair of warlocks.

And now I'm holding my mate in my arms with my cock up his ass.

Congo smiled as he licked absently at the back of Zhaul's neck. Never had he experienced such exquisite sensations as the ones his mate had granted him. Zhaul's ass was truly the stuff of legends.

"Mmmm," Zhaul hummed, turning his head to peer at him over his shoulder. "Still hard?" He chuckled roughly as he clenched his chute gently. "How's that possible?"

Shrugging one shoulder, Congo tightened his arms, keeping Zhaul snug to his chest. He couldn't help himself. Once he'd sunk his erection deep, deep into Zhaul's body, Congo couldn't resist feeling that exquisite heat as often—and for as long—as possible.

"I did warn you," Congo murmured. "I plan to stay right here." He ground his hips against Zhaul's ass. "A lot."

Hell, it wasn't even about fucking.

Congo didn't need to get off. He'd already orgasmed three times in the last hour. Between fucking Zhaul into the mattress before exchanging claiming bites once more, he'd filled his lover's channel twice. Then Congo had adjusted their position, spooned up behind his mate, and slipped back inside him.

53

After a slow, easy ride, sending them both soaring once again, Congo had curled around Zhaul and never pulled out. He didn't feel the need. It felt too good to stay connected with his mate.

"I like it," Zhaul admitted.

Congo lifted his head and pecked a kiss to Zhaul's offered lips. "Good."

Then Congo settled back on the pillow, his nose pressed against his mate's nape. His lover smelled so good. Flicking out his tongue, Congo licked a bead of salt from his skin.

Tastes damn fantastic, too.

"How are you doing?"

Surprised at the question, Congo paused to give the question its due. How was he doing? Humming, Congo nuzzled his nose in Zhaul's gorgeous dark hair, enjoying the feel of the strands on his face.

"Well, I'm as free as possible, at the moment," Congo mused slowly. "Which is a damn sight better than when I woke this morning." Lifting his head again, Congo nipped at Zhaul's shoulder. "And I have my mate in my arms." Sliding the hand on his lover's hip up his body, he gently cupped Zhaul's jaw and urged him to turn his head once more. Congo met his mate's honey-brown eyes and smiled. "I'm doing damn fantastic, Zhaul."

After pecking another kiss to Zhaul's lips, Congo relaxed back again. "Tell me about yourself," he urged. "Where's your sleuth from?"

Zhaul tensed in his arms a little, and Congo tried to decide why that would upset him. Rubbing his palm over his mate's chest, he did his best to soothe his mate. Recalling that Zhaul had been kidnapped while trying to get laid — and forcing his bear to relax, the panda shifter was theirs now — Congo wondered if the man had a sleuth.

"Were you a loan panda?" Congo asked softly. Squeezing his mate in his arms, he stated, "You'll never be alone again.

My sleuth isn't much at the moment, but you're one of us now."

"I had a sleuth," Zhaul softly revealed. "A small one in Indiana." Before Congo could come up with how to address that, Zhaul added, "When I was kidnapped six months ago, no one reported me missing to the Shifter Council."

"Damn," Congo growled, suddenly feeling the need to go kick someone's ass. "Why the hell not?"

Even though Congo and his people had been a small, off-the-grid community, they still knew how to contact the Shifter Council.

"I don't know," Zhaul replied, sounding sad. "I would have thought that at least my mother or brother would have found a way, but they didn't."

"Maybe we'll have to take a ride out that way and find out," Congo offered, rubbing Zhaul's chest and nuzzling his neck. "Figure out what happened."

Zhaul shook his head. "I'm not sure I want to." Turning his head again, he met Congo's gaze. "What if they didn't report me because they just didn't care?"

While Congo understood that fear, he wanted the sadness out of Zhaul's scent, too. "Was your alpha an asshole? Maybe they didn't let them." Seeing the way his mate nibbled his bottom lip, Congo asked, "What did you do in your sleuth? You don't strike me as the big, dominant, enforcer type."

Oh, no. With the way Zhaul had cared for him, Congo would bet his bottom dollar — if he had one, which he didn't — that his mate was the kind-hearted nurturing type. As far as Congo was concerned, that was perfect for him. His sleuth had been through so much. They needed nurturing, and Congo really wasn't the bear to do it.

Which is why Zhaul is so perfect, not just for me, but for my sleuth.

"I was the local barber and stylist," Zhaul admitted, his cheeks taking on a pinkish hue while embarrassment filled his scent. "I owned a shop in our small town."

"Ah." Congo pinned his mate with his most impressed and appreciative smile. "That explains how you knew how to shave me. Gods, that felt so damn good." Pecking a kiss to Zhaul's lips, Congo whispered, "Thank you, my mate. I can't remember the last time I was so pampered. I loved it."

Zhaul's relief came through in his scent and smile. "I'm glad you enjoyed it."

"I did," Congo confirmed again. "Very much."

Clearing his throat, Zhaul admitted, "And my alpha wasn't very impressed with me, but he didn't really say anything." His eyes narrowing, he admitted, "There was definitely an exasperated look or ten when I'd do something, uh . . . feminine, in his opinion." Shrugging, Zhaul stated, "Guess he doesn't consider cutting people's hair a very masculine profession."

"Douchebag," Congo stated with a scoff. "Shows what he knows. The barber profession started with men."

To Congo's pleasure, Zhaul snickered. "Maybe I'll just try calling first," he said after a moment of silence. "Or a video chat. Then I could see her expression." Resting his hand over Congo's wrist, Zhaul squeezed it lightly. "I'm not ready to leave Kontra's people, yet, and I can't imagine you are either."

While following the orders of another bear, even a grizzly, wasn't Congo's style, he knew Zhaul was right. "They are the best chance we have to break this blasted spell, once and for all," he mused with a sigh.

Zhaul nodded. "They'll get it done." Then he cleared his throat and asked, "After that, will you go back to the Catskills?"

Congo immediately shook his head. "No, our location was compromised." Scoffing, he frowned as he added, "I don't even know if the property is still in our name. It's been almost three years."

"Lamar will be able to check into that for you," Zhaul told

him. "He's really good at research on computers." Whispering softly, he admitted, "He was able to let me know that the bank foreclosed on my shop, since I was no longer there." With what sounded like forced happiness, Zhaul added, "At least my cottage is still mine. My grandparents left it to me free and clear, and annual taxes aren't due for another few months."

"I'm sorry," Congo replied instinctively. "How did they die?"

"Oh, they didn't." Zhaul smiled over his shoulder at him. "They had just been living so long in the area that their lack of aging was starting to get noticed, so they faked their death, leaving the house to me." Sighing, Zhaul told him, "They moved to a sleuth in Missouri."

"So you could possibly contact them, too?" Congo offered. "Perhaps they're missing you."

Zhaul nodded, his tone turning vacant. "Maybe."

Congo guessed there was a story there, but before he could ask, Zhaul continued, "What about you? Is Madagascar your only brother?"

"Only brother who still talks to me," Congo admitted. While he still felt a hint of frustration and sadness when thinking of his family, there wasn't nearly the pain he'd once harbored. "I have two more brothers. One older and another younger. Kenya and Chad. When I was kicked out of my sleuth for being gay, Madagascar went with me, and they stopped talking to either of us."

"I'm so sorry," Zhaul immediately told him. Then, to Congo's surprise, he snorted. "I-I'm so sorry." He smiled over his shoulder at him. "Did you just say your brothers are Kenya and Chad?" When Congo nodded, Zhaul's smile widened to a grin. "And you're Congo and Madagascar?"

Rolling his eyes, Congo realized what Zhaul had noticed. "Yes, we're all named after places in Africa."

Zhaul snorted before clapping a hand over his mouth.

Enjoying the moment of levity—their conversation had ended up way too serious, which had caused Congo's dick to soften, even if he hadn't pulled out, yet—Congo grumbled, "Laugh it up. Get it out of your system." He made certain to keep some amusement in his voice, so Zhaul would know he wasn't actually upset with him.

"What'd she do?" Zhaul teased with a snort. "Throw darts at a map of Africa?"

"It's entirely possible," Congo admitted with a shrug. "She wasn't very maternal."

For a moment, Congo listened to Zhaul's snickers and snorts. He smiled against his mate's neck, enjoying the sound of his laughter, even if it was sort of at his expense. The sound and scent of his mate's happiness even caused his wilted erection to firm back up. When it had gone on for several minutes, Congo grinned and nipped at Zhaul's shoulder.

"Okay, that's enough of that," Congo mock growled. He pushed Zhaul forward, forcing him to roll onto his stomach. Congo followed the move, ending up on Zhaul's back, so he didn't have to pull out. "Naughty mate, laughing at me." Congo lightly smacked the side of Zhaul's ass cheek. "Time for your punishment."

Then Congo pulled partway out, only to reverse directions and slam into his lover.

Zhaul immediately moaned, trying to arch underneath him.

Congo didn't allow it. He threaded his fingers with Zhaul's and pressed most of his weight on his lover, pinning him to the mattress. Then, moving only his hips, he began a swift thrust and retreat, driving into his mate over and over again.

The sounds of Zhaul's whimpering groans, his pleas for more, and his rough calling of Congo's name told him that he pegged his lover's gland with each rut.

Yup, those sounds are even better than his laughter.

CHAPTER NINE

Zhaul took Congo's hand and led his mate from the bed-room. As much as he would have loved to stay holed up in their room for the duration of the afternoon, when he'd heard his mate's stomach growling, he'd known it was time to come out. His lover was already underweight. He needed feeding.

Heading downstairs, Zhaul turned away from the front door and moved deeper into the home. He pushed open a sliding door on the right to reveal a large dining room. A quick glance showed eight people at the table, including four that were Congo's bears, now in human form. They appeared to have taken showers, and three of them were now clean-shaven. The fourth, who looked an awful lot like Congo, sported a goatee.

That man lifted his focus away from his heaping plate of food and grinned broadly at them. "Congo, congratulations!" He rose from his chair and crossed to them, his arms wide. "What a fantastic day, huh?"

Congo wrapped the man in his arms and returned his back-slapping hug. "That it is, Mads. That it is."

Due to Congo swiftly unwinding one arm, Zhaul managed to fight back his bear's growl.

As if understanding, Congo moved one hand to Mads' nape while wrapping his other around Zhaul. He hauled him close and stated, "Zhaul, this is my brother, Madagascar."

Oh, right. His brother. I've seen him before.

Then Congo grinned at Madagascar. "Mads, this is my

59

mate, Zhaul." As if extremely proud, Congo released Madagascar's neck in order to tug aside the top of his t-shirt. "He
claimed me."

Madagascar roared with obvious pleasure, a wide grin
splitting his features. "My big brother's been claimed," he
cried joyously. Wrapping his arms around them both, Madagascar declared, "I have a new brother. Welcome to the sleuth,
Zhaul."

Shocked at the male's exuberance, Zhaul struggled to find
his tongue. "Th-Thanks," he squeaked, knowing his eyes had
to be as big as saucers.

Releasing them, Madagascar turned to the others at the table. "Did you hear that, guys? Our alpha has been claimed!"

The three still sitting leaped to their feet, tipped their heads
back, and roared their pleasure to the ceiling.

Zhaul gaped, having never seen anything like it.

Then all three of them hurried forward to offer congratulations and hugs. They introduced themselves as Valentine,
Zion, and Eurik.

"Where's Shannon?" Congo asked, glancing between his
men.

"He was finishing up his shower when I headed down
here," Zion told him. "I'll go get him." Then he rushed from
the room.

"I didn't mean to interrupt your meal, guys." Congo
pointed at the table. "Sit back down and finish." He focused
on Zhaul and asked, "Should we go in the kitchen and make
ourselves something?"

"No need," a black man at the table called—Mutegi, if
Zhaul remembered correctly. There were a lot of gang members. "Ben and I"—he rested his hand over that of the dark-
haired human's sitting next to him—"as well as Caleb and
Emmett"—he indicated the other pair at the table—"have
been cooking up a storm." Touching his chest with his free

hand, he claimed, "I am Mutegi. If you need anything, please feel free to ask." He smiled, showing off even white teeth in his black face. "There is plenty."

"And more where that came from," Caleb assured with a grin. "We're just sitting here taking a break while we wait for you guys to eat some of what we've already made." With a laugh, he added, "Then we'll make even more and start taking plates out to the others. It's an army out there."

Zhaul had noticed that, too. The gang was huge. When he'd been stuck in animal form, waiting for the scientists' drugs to wear off, Yuma had told him all about the gang.

Originally, there had been only a dozen guys, all single, driving around the country as a motorcycle gang. One by one, they'd begun finding their mates. Some of the guys had settled with their other half, but many more of them had stayed on the road with Kontra.

Even the ones left behind were still considered family. Occasionally, they dropped by to ride with them for a week or two before returning home.

"Thanks, Caleb." Grabbing Congo's hand again, Zhaul led them through the archway to the kitchen. He spotted huge warming trays spread across a much smaller table. They were full of many different types of food, from tuna pasta casserole to funeral potatoes to grilled chicken strips.

"Oh, damn," Congo rumbled, drifting toward the food. "That all looks and smells so good."

His stomach rumbled again, and Zhaul saw the longing in his mate's eyes. Turning to the left, he opened a cupboard and grabbed two plates. "Here." He handed both to the other man, then snagged a couple more plates for himself. With a grin, Zhaul started toward the feast. "Dig in."

Zhaul led by example and started filling his plates. He took two large pieces of fried chicken, a scoop of tuna pasta salad, and a few other things. He heaped a salad onto his other plate, then topped it with several strips of grilled chicken. Finally, Zhaul doused that in creamy Caesar dressing.

When Zhaul was done, he noticed with pleasure that Congo had filled both his plates, too. They were near to overflowing, and if Zhaul had to guess, his mate had taken some of just about everything.

"We'll put these in the dining room, then come back for drinks," Zhaul told him.

"They don't stand on ceremony here, huh?" Congo whispered as he followed Zhaul.

Zhaul shook his head. He'd only eaten a few meals with the gang, but everyone had always been really laid back. They shared everything and worked as a team.

Except —

"Just don't touch any of the motorcycles without permission," Zhaul counseled with a smirk. "That's the only thing they're pretty possessive about."

Congo chuckled. "Understandable. Used to ride one myself, but I sold it when me and a few guys opened up the compound in the mountains." He shrugged, but his expression appeared a little wistful. "Just no use for it, and we needed the money for building supplies."

Zhaul bumped his shoulder into Congo's. "Maybe we'll buy a couple someday," he told him with a smile. "I've never ridden one before."

"You've never ridden a motorcycle?" Congo sounded surprised.

Setting his plates on the table, Zhaul shook his head. "Nope."

"You're totally missing out," Caleb told him as he rose to his feet. "You guys sit and get started. What would you like to drink? We have just about everything from juice to spirits."

Congo groaned from next to him, licking his lips. "Damn, I'd love a beer." His expression appeared so hopeful. "I couldn't even give a shit what kind."

Chuckling, Caleb gave him a thumbs up. "You got it." He focused on Zhaul as he asked, "What about you, Zhaul? Want iced tea again or to try something different?"

Having spotted the wine rack while getting food, Zhaul asked, "Is there any white wine open?" He grinned as he looked Congo's way. "We're celebrating."

"That you are," Caleb agreed, heading into the kitchen. "A cold beer and a glass of white coming right up."

It wasn't until Zhaul had taken his first bite of food that he realized Caleb hadn't answered the question about the wine already being open.

Oh well.

Zhaul scooped up a forkful of mashed potatoes and gravy, slipped it into his mouth, and hummed appreciatively.

At some point during the meal, Shannon had arrived, Zion returning with him. The bear shifter had exclaimed just as jovially, pulling each of them into a hug. Then he'd grabbed a plate of food and joined them.

As they ate, they explained how each of them had found their way to Congo and Madagascar's secluded mountain compound. The conversation grew a bit subdued when Zion shared how his parents had died, so he'd grown up with his mother's family. When the sleuth had been found by hunters targeting paranormals, many of them had been slaughtered. Zion and his cousin, Acadia, had fled into the woods. They'd stumbled upon Congo's compound by accident but were forever grateful that he'd taken them in.

Zhaul took a sip of his wine, trying to come up with some way to lift the mood.

Alpha Kontra's appearance caught everyone's attention. The huge bear shifter swept his gaze over them. Smiling, he pinned his attention on Zhaul and Congo.

"Congratulations on completing your mating, guys." Leaning against the wall, he shoved his hands into the pockets of his jeans. "I'm very happy for you." Then he paused, his brows furrowing, as if working through how to bring something up. Kontra clicked his tongue once before shaking his head. "This is hard because I don't want anything I say to sound like an order."

Understanding his predicament, Zhaul offered, "What if you spoke directly to me?" Seeing the way Kontra arched his brow in silent question, he quickly explained his idea. "That way, they could hear but won't be compelled to follow your words as if they were a command."

Kontra nodded once. "Sounds like a good plan." Crooking his finger, he motioned for Zhaul to come to him. Once Zhaul stood before him, Kontra told him, "If this doesn't work, Zhaul, I'll need to know."

Zhaul knew that the comment wasn't meant for him alone, even if he was the only one being addressed. Still, he dutifully responded, "Yes, Alpha."

"Good."

Even though Zhaul found it a little unnerving, he continued to stand before the alpha, waiting for whatever he had to say.

Resting a hand on Zhaul's nape, Kontra once again massaged lightly, soothing him. "Famine passed on Zion's request to his brothers, Death and War. Both are coming here soon." His brown-eyed gaze stared at him steadily. "Death is bringing one prisoner. War is bringing two. If your mate's sleuth would like a hand in the restitution, then they'll need to be outside in thirty minutes."

Zion's growl caught everyone's attention. His nearly black eyes were narrowed, and anger glittered within their depths. "Thank you, Alpha Kontra," he rumbled. "I'll be there."

"As will I," Congo stated, rising to his feet. He peered around at the others. "Know this. There is no shame if you decide you don't want to face your persecutors. You can tell me privately your thoughts on restitution."

One by one, each bear shifter declared that they would be there, ready and willing to face those who'd tortured and subjugated them.

Zhaul could see the pride in Congo's eyes, smell it in his scent, as he smiled at each of those who remained of his sleuth. Returning to his mate's side, he slipped his hand into his mate's. When Congo turned his attention on him, Zhaul grinned at him.

"I'll be there, too," Zhaul whispered.

Congo wrapped him in his arms and hugged him tightly. Dipping his head, he whispered, "I don't want you anywhere near those bitches." Before Zhaul could growl his annoyance at all but being ordered to stay away, Congo continued, "But I would be honored to have you at my side, my mate."

Squeezing Congo tightly, Zhaul murmured back, "I'll always be at your side."

After inhaling deeply, letting it out just as slowly, then kissing the claiming mark he'd left on Zhaul's neck, Congo lifted his head and nodded. "Okay, then." He turned his attention to Alpha Kontra. "We'll be right out."

"Finish your—" Kontra snapped his mouth shut and shook his head. Then he forced a smile and amended, "It would be perfectly acceptable for you to finish your meal before joining us outside." Then Kontra grinned broadly at Mutegi. "You know what, Mutegi. I think we need to make this look like a celebration. Let those bitches know they don't scare us."

"I'll tap the keg!" Payson yelled, running through the room. "Come on, Land."

Zhaul watched as Payson's human mate—he didn't know where either had been hiding, having so obviously been eavesdropping—giggled as he sprinted after his crazy hyena shifter.

Mutegi chuckled even as he shook his head. The others laughed, and even Kontra rumbled a snort of amusement.

"Come on, guys," Emmett encouraged, rising from his seat. "Let's get some tables set up outside, the barbeque started, and a bonfire lit."

Caleb snickered. "We could pretend that we plan to burn the witches at the stake."

"Not a bad restitution, come to think of it," Zion grumbled.

As the others snorted, obviously amused, Zhaul noticed Shannon looked a little pale at the idea.

Zhaul couldn't say he was too interested in learning what the smell of burning flesh was, either.

As they all took their plates outside to finish their meal, Zhaul wondered if he was the only one who'd lost his appetite.

CHAPTER TEN

W ithin fifteen minutes, Kontra's people had set up chairs, tables, tents, and the vast array of food trays had been moved outside. The grill had been started, a bonfire lit, and there were plenty of camping chairs. The scent of grilling meat filled the air.

Congo's stomach was so tied up in knots that he didn't think he would be able to eat a damn thing. Only with Zhaul's continued encouragement did he manage to finish what had been on the plate he'd carried out. He made a mental note to go in and place the dirty one he'd left on the table into the dishwasher . . . assuming there was one.

"Relax, Congo," Payson urged, flopping onto a nearby camping chair. He grabbed Land and pulled the human onto his lap. "We're really, really good at this."

As Congo watched, Payson took one of the beers Land had been holding. Land held a second out to him. After a second of hesitation, Congo took it, seeing as he'd drained his first.

"Good at what?" Zion asked curiously. The bear shifter sat on the ground, his legs crossed before him, and was steadily making his way through several pieces of fried chicken. Evidently, seeing the witches pay for their crimes gave Zion an appetite.

Congo's other bears were clustered around them, either sitting in chairs or opting for the ground like Zion.

"Good at making people pay for their crimes," Land told them, taking a sip of the white wine that Zhaul had declined with a soft reply of, *I'll get some more in a bit.* Then Land's nose wrinkled, and at first, Congo thought it was because he didn't like the wine. Then Land pointed out, "Although, technically, this time, I think it's the horsemen who stopped the witches and are making them pay."

"As long as it gets done," Zion began around a mouthful of food. "I don't give a shit who does it."

"Here, here!" Payson lifted his beer in salute to Zion, who grinned and nodded in response. After swallowing a mouthful, he hummed and peered around as if searching for someone. "I think one of them is here."

"You're very perceptive, little hyena," a deep rumbly voice came from behind him.

Payson snickered while squinting, as if that would make it easier to see whoever—probably a horseman. "Who you callin' little, dude?"

"Weeell." The male drew the word out for a heartbeat. Then he appeared, and Congo damn near fell off his chair. "I *am* a lot bigger than you."

That was an understatement. A hulking male stood before them. He sported skin dark as midnight with muscles upon muscles. His eyes were blood red, he had red horns atop his head, and huge red bat-like wings billowed behind him.

"You must be War." Payson didn't seem fazed at all. Instead, he grinned broadly as he eyed War up and down, who bowed grandly as if accepting an overture. "Hey, can I touch your wings?"

War tipped his head back and laughed. "Sure." He brought one forward, dangling it before Payson.

"Sweet." Payson immediately began petting the appendage. "So much softer than I thought it'd be." He gripped it and pushed it toward Land. "Check it out."

After a few seconds and a covert look at War, Land touched the appendage, too.

Congo could only stare in shock at the brazen pair.

Chuckling, War tugged his wing away from them, saying, "Unlike with gargoyles and even a few demons, a horseman's wings are not sexual." With a wink, he started toward the bonfire where Kontra stood with several others. War called over his shoulder, his gaze meeting Congo's, "They make fantastic weapons in battle, though."

"I guess I should have taken that drink after all," Zhaul whispered.

Absently, unable to tear his gaze away from War's massive frame, Congo held out his beer bottle to Zhaul.

Not surprisingly, Zhaul took it.

A second later, another male arrived—pale and slender, wearing a black cloak and carrying a scythe.

Death he recognized.

After a few words together, Kontra pointed in Congo's direction. They all headed toward Congo and his group. Stopping a few feet away, War gave them another wide smile. Death swept his gaze over them, appearing somewhat relieved.

"I'm pleased to see you well," Death told them, his relief obvious. "Even though I've been told that you're still struggling with some . . . after-effects."

Unable to help himself, Congo scoffed. "Well, if by after-effects, with some very careful wording, the only orders we're spell-bound to follow are Kontra's . . . yeah, we're doing much better."

War grunted, resting his hands on his hips. "It could be worse," he pointed out. "You could still be under the witch circle's control."

Congo nodded. "True enough."

Clapping his hands together, War glanced between them. "So, I understand in the paranormal culture, restitution is in order." Then War scowled as he added, "Uh, I'm not certain how it applies in this case, unless you intend to inflict every-thing on them that they did to you."

"Watching their deaths will suffice," Congo stated coldly. "We just need to know they can't ever return."

"Not me," Zion rumbled on a snarl. "I plan to be the exe-cutioner." A feral anger bled into his voice as his scent turned sour. "They cost me the only blood family I have. I want vengeance."

"Fair enough," Death responded, not at all sounding sur-prised or taken aback. "Their lives are yours."

Zion grunted with acceptance.

A second later, three figures appeared — two large black demons standing on either side of a bound female. There was a hood on the woman, and she swayed. The male on the right gripped her upper arm, holding her up.

In the next instant, six more people appeared. They stood a few paces to the first trio's left. There were four demon guards and two bound females. One woman drooped against one of the guards, appearing unconscious. The second woman stood straight and tall, her stance screaming her defi-ance. Once again, they wore hoods.

Setting his plate aside, Zion rose to his feet, brushing off the seat of his pants as he went.

Congo rose as well and moved toward Zion, lending his support to his clearly angry sleuth-member. He rested his hand on his friend's shoulder, squeezing lightly. Feeling his mate step up next to him, Congo wished he could keep the man back, but he knew asking would just annoy his lover.

"Let's go meet the witches," Congo rumbled, glancing be-tween Death and War.

Both horsemen dipped their chin in nods. Then they turned and led the way.

After Congo had taken a few steps, he glanced behind him.

While all of his bears had risen to their feet, three had expectant looks on their faces. Shannon shifted from foot to foot while rubbing the back of his neck.

Congo made a mental note to speak with Shannon soon, perhaps try to help him settle. He was clearly having a tough time with something.

Stopping before the group, War flicked his fingers. All three of the hoods were yanked off. He felt his heart skip a beat as he recognized all of them.

The haughty blonde on the left was one of the ones who'd cut sigils into their backs. The other two, brunettes, had been there chanting, lending strength to the spells. While one dark-haired woman looked around in fear, the other, plus the blonde, glared with hatred at them. The blonde's gaze even held contempt, her lip curling with obvious scorn, even around her ball-gag.

"Lisa Melbram, Connie Espie, and Winoan Rouldran," Death toned solemnly. "You have all been found guilty in the kidnapping and subjugation of shifters, resulting in many deaths. How do you plead?"

For a few seconds, no one spoke.

Unable to help his curiosity, Congo murmured, "How are they supposed to answer while gagged?"

"Oh, we broke through the spells they were using to shield their minds," War replied, a growl in his tone. He pinned his attention on the blonde. "We can read their minds." War's eyes narrowed. "And what you just said, Lisa. Not nice."

Lisa responded by growling and trying to shout through the ball-gag.

Death stepped back and swung his hand toward them, his focus falling on Zion. "They are yours to dispatch as you please."

Even as Zion whipped his shirt over his head, obviously preparing to shift, a bolt of light streaked out of the trees and slammed into the shifter's chest. Zion flew backward, landed with a thud, and slid several feet across the dirt.

Congo tackled Zhaul to the ground. At the same time, the demons spread their wings and chanted. The next shot slammed into a shield and crackled around them for a few seconds before the energy dissipated.

Peering Zion's way, Congo felt a measure of relief when he spotted his chest rise and fall. Doctor Eli seemed to appear out of nowhere, dropping beside the downed bear. Shifters shot in all directions, in both human and animal form.

The horsemen were nowhere to be seen.

Except, as Congo watched, he never scented panic or heard screams. Instead, there were roars of challenge and swift animals streaking into the woods — *toward* where the shots were being fired from.

Just as swiftly as it started, the attack ended. A naked Kontra exited the trees, flanked by an equally nude Sam — his beta and a Texas longhorn bull shifter — as well as Mutegi and Payson, who were still in animal form.

"Zion okay?" Kontra immediately asked, his gaze falling upon him.

Eli nodded. "Looks like a stunning spell," he revealed. His dark eyes glittered with anger. "Seems they were trying to retake him . . . and perhaps more of us."

"I wanna know how the fuck they knew where we are," Kontra bellowed. "Get me some information. *Now!*"

"Someone called them," Draven replied, slipping from between another set of trees. He shoved a gagged woman before him and held up a cell phone. "From Payson's number."

"What?" Kontra scowled as he glanced from Payson in hyena form — who snarled in anger — back to Draven. "Who?"

Draven shrugged. "Don't know."

"I'll let you know," War claimed, stalking from the forest. He dragged an unconscious woman in one hand and a young male acolyte in the other. The human whimpered, clutching the witch's herb satchel to his chest when War dropped them both ceremoniously to the ground. Lifting his palm, War twitched his fingers in a *gimme* motion. "Give her here." The young man rolled to his belly, making as if to crawl away. Lifting his clawed foot, War landed it on the human's back. "Stay there, asshole."

"Don't hurt him!" Shannon screamed, streaking across the yard. He skidded to a stop, sliding to the ground. A clearly surprised War lifted his foot when Shannon grabbed the man and tucked him against his chest in a protective embrace. "Please, don't hurt him."

Congo helped Zhaul to his feet before they both headed toward Shannon and the man he held — protected. "Shannon, what's going on?"

"I did it," Shannon admitted, anguish filling his voice as he glanced around at everyone. "I called them. I had to." His voice broke as he repeated, "I had to."

Even as Congo's gut twisted uncomfortably, he demanded, "Why, Shannon? Why would you call the goddamned witches and tell them where we are?" As Congo continued to question his sleuth-member, he couldn't help how his voice rose in volume.

Shannon's actions had put not only Zhaul in danger but the other sleuth-members as well . . . not to mention everyone else.

Sorrow flooding Shannon's dark eyes, he pinned his gaze on Congo. "He's my mate," he whispered. After a glance down at the man curled up and trembling in his arms, who still refused to lift his head, Shannon darted his gaze around the group. "This is Evan. Evan Reyes. He's my mate. I-I-I had no way to find him." Shannon turned pleading eyes on Congo once more. "Evan became an acolyte for the witches a year and a half ago. I had to rescue him from their perversity."

"You met your mate a year and a half ago, and you couldn't do anything about it?" Zhaul's quietly rumbled question was filled with quiet sympathy. "I'm so sorry."

"Well, shit," Kontra grumbled, crossing his arms over his chest. "Guess I understand why you did it." Shaking his head, he muttered, "Just wish you would have come to us to help instead of giving up our location."

"You owe Zion and anyone else who was injured restitution," Congo declared, frustration swelling through him. Rubbing his hand over his face, he turned his attention to Kontra and shrugged helplessly. "I'm sorry. I'm sorry we put you and your people in danger."

Sure, Congo understood Shannon's actions, too, but there most definitely had to have been a better way. The entire sleuth—hell, probably most of Kontra's gang—would have helped discover Evan's whereabouts. Instead, Shannon had gone off half-cocked and created problems for them all.

Kontra sighed heavily, resting his hand on Congo's shoulders. "We're always in danger, and we can handle it." Then he scowled at Shannon. "Take Evan to a room upstairs," he ordered. "We're going to need to talk to him."

Shannon looked beyond relieved and quickly rose to his feet. Tucking the whimpering human to his chest, he started away. He paused after a few steps and looked back at them.

"I-I'm sorry," Shannon whispered, anguish on his features. "I just—" He shrugged, his lips twisting into a grimace. "Sorry," Shannon muttered again before rushing away.

After Shannon had disappeared, Kontra rumbled, "Don't worry, Congo. We'll deal with this. We'll be safe." His eyes narrowed, and a low growl rumbled from him even as his smile held an aggressive surety. "We're not alone in this. Not anymore." Then Kontra sobered. "But if you feel the need to be sent to a new location, I'll see that it's done."

Congo hesitated an instant as he searched out the faces of

his sleuth-members. The other three wore grim smiles. Madagascar offered him a crooked grin as he indicated the guys around them with his chin.

Getting it, Congo returned his gaze to Kontra. "No. We're where we want to be right now . . . if you'll still have us."

When Congo felt Zhaul squeeze his side, Congo knew he'd made the right choice in his request.

Kontra smiled warmly as he nodded. "I'm glad to hear it."

Before Congo could come up with anything else to say, Death stalked from the forest. He, too, dragged an unconscious woman. Tossing her at their feet, the horseman grinned broadly.

"It wasn't all for naught." Death held up a thick tome that appeared to be covered in a red leather hide. "They had The Red Book on them."

War scoffed, his grin wide and creepy. "Well, thank fuck for that."

ABOUT THE AUTHOR

Charlie started writing fantasy when she was eight, and after stumbling onto her first erotic romance at age nineteen, she realized her true calling. She now focuses on writing gay erotic romance, normally of the paranormal variety, with heroes of all kinds. With the help and support of her husband, Charlie finally fulfilled one of her life-long goals . . . move to acreage with her horses. You can often find her curled up with her laptop and a cup of tea or glass of wine, creating her next adventure. Charlie enjoys exploring the mountains of her new Oregon home on horseback, 4-wheeler, or motorcycle.

She can be reached at ch.richards2010@yahoo.com
Or visit her at www.charlie-richards.com